What Happens In Vegas
A Spicy Comedy Novella
Cheryl Terra

bang it out
WR TINC

Bang It Out Writing

Author's Note

Please note that this books is written in Canadian English, which has rules and spellings from both UK and US English.

I have tried to address any potential triggers here as best I can without providing spoilers, but if you have concerns about any of the items listed and wish to know more, please reach out to me via email at **info@che rylterra.com**.

This book is intended for adults and features sexually explicit scenes that contain dirty talk and first time sex/losing virginity. The adult entertainment industry and certain issues surrounding it feature heavily in this book, as does a character who has illegally immigrated to the US.

A cheating relationship occurs in this book, though not between or by the main characters. There are mild scenes featuring attempted sexual harassment, homophobia, alcoholism, childhood trauma featuring emotional abuse, and minor slut shaming.

ONE

HAD I KNOWN I was going to see the man of my dreams for the first time that day, I would have dressed differently.

Well, not *dressed* differently, I guess. A uniform is a uniform and a low-cut black t-shirt is a low-cut black t-shirt. I suppose I could have worn different denim shorts. I'd gone for Bermuda length instead of the ones that Dante preferred, which were supposed to hit just a little higher than mid-thigh. And they did on most girls, I guess, but that length spilled firmly into the territory of short-shorts on a girl as tall and curvy as me.

So I guess I couldn't have dressed differently, but I still could have looked like I was trying a little harder. Like, I could have kept my hair down instead of in the two utilitarian French braids I wore most days since I hated how round my face looked when I put it up in a ponytail. My hair was the most stereotypical shade of red; not the sunny strawberry-kissed blonde or fiery ruby or rich auburn that people pictured when they thought of a sultry redhead, but the quintessential carroty ginger that people thought of when they joked about being dropped off by the milkman.

But maybe if I'd let Rico at it with his curling iron and clouds of hairspray like he kept asking to do, I would have looked less like a sturdy, broad-shouldered milkmaid and more like someone who would capture *his* eye the way he'd captured mine.

Maybe if I would have done my makeup, it would have covered the countless freckles scattered across the white skin of my nose and cheeks. Though, it would have done nothing for the ones that trailed down my chest and back and arms. But he might not have noticed those ones if I contoured myself some cheekbones and plumped my pout into puffy, pillowy, pink lips and had big, thick eyelashes to simper under as I looked up at him.

So long as I was seated, anyway.

Because he wasn't tall. An inch or two taller than me, maybe, but nowhere near "gazing up at him through my eyelashes" height. But that was a good thing, since every inch of him was already unfairly beautiful. Adding more height would have just made him even more unattainable.

His arms got me first: thick and toned and encased by the t-shirt hugging his biceps, with black and grey tattoos snaking down his left arm all the way to his wrist. That same t-shirt was fitted around his chest, showing off the obvious muscles beneath. And somehow, he made a pair of baggy grey cargo shorts one of the hottest things I'd ever seen before. There were tattoos on both of his calves—a butterfly on the left and a scorpion on the right, both in the same monochrome style as the ones on his arms—and possibly one more on his ankle, though he was wearing dark socks beneath the Converse low-tops he had on, so I couldn't tell if—

"And his *name*?" Rico asked, shaking me from the reverie as I described *him*.

"Huh?"

Rico laughed. "Oh, Miss Violet, you're head over heels already, aren't you?"

"I wouldn't say that. I mean, he was just... hot."

"Mm-hmm," Rico said, drawing out the *mmm* sarcastically. "You see hot guys all the time. No one makes you react like this."

"I just thought you'd appreciate hearing about how hot he is."

"You know I do. I just don't know that I've ever seen you get all misty over some sexy bearded bartender with tattoos and muscles before."

"All misty?"

"I was going to say 'misty-eyed,' but I don't know if it's your eyes or your panties that are mistier."

"You're disgusting," I said, but I couldn't stop myself from laughing.

Rico grinned and nudged me. "So? Come on, *chica*. There were hardly any prospects for me at the club tonight. I need to live vicariously through you. What's Mr. Making-You-Misty's name?"

I twisted my mouth to the side. "Well, the thing about that is..."

Rico stared down at me. Not in a condescending way. I had my head resting on his thigh as we lounged on the couch after we'd each completed our jobs for the day. He was gently working my hair out of its braids and glancing at his phone every so often, which probably meant he'd been messaging a new guy on Grindr and was hoping for a late-night booty call. But I knew he'd sit there as long as I needed regardless of if he got a booty call or not, because Rico was awesome like that.

There was a lot I wouldn't have if it wasn't for Rico. A place to live, for one. Or any friends at all. And my hair would still look flat and stringy like it had when I first moved to Vegas. He'd taken me under his wing after realizing I was entirely hopeless and out of my element after one of his late-night booty calls a few months earlier.

Not with me. No, Rico's booty call had been with my boyfriend.

I'd known Trevor was bi. That's what he'd told me, anyway. I mean, we moved to Vegas together because he was completely dedicated to drag. He had insisted there was no way he could manage to further his career as a drag queen in the small Saskatchewan town we'd grown up

3

in. That was fair, though I still wasn't entirely sure why he picked Las Vegas over somewhere like Toronto or Vancouver so we didn't need to leave Canada.

But he'd been insistent on Las Vegas. So at twenty-one, I'd quit my job at the grocery store and snuck across the border with him, thinking that when he said we should wait to have sex until we were married, that we'd eventually... you know.

Get married.

Not that he was trying to cover up the fact that he wasn't at all into women.

But I was an unobservant idiot sometimes, so I believed it. Right up until we were strolling down the Strip together one night a month or two after moving to Vegas and a decadently tall drag queen spotted us and waved excitedly.

"Trevor! Hey *papi*!" she said.

I smiled. That had to be good, right? Trevor was there to do drag, and a drag queen recognized him... that was good. But before I could be too proud of him, Trevor's face went *white*.

I saw him glance from left to right, as if he was trying to decide if hurtling over the fence onto the boulevard or into the Bellagio fountain would be worth it. But the queen had started towards us, impossibly fast even though she was wearing heels that I would have probably broken my ankle in, and Trevor didn't even have time to remember that he could turn around and bolt in the other direction.

"Um... hey," he replied weakly.

I was still kind of a moron, so I smiled at the queen as she came up and planted a kiss on Trevor's cheek, leaving behind a big smear of fuschia lipstick. She lifted a manicured finger and booped him on the nose with a loud laugh.

"How have you been?" she asked. "I'm finally walking straight again, thank you for asking, Mr. Monster."

Trevor made a noise that the queen must have thought was a laugh, but he didn't say anything. After a moment, she winked at me.

"It's always the shy, skinny ones that surprise you," she said. "Hello, beautiful. Look at you with that red hair. You're stunning. I'm Faye Laytio—since as Trevor can tell you, that's my specialty—but he would've probably told you he was screaming 'Rico! Rico!' last weekend."

I wasn't enough of a moron to think they were playing video games or talking drag or something.

"You did what?" I asked, turning to Trevor.

He winced. "Violet, wait, it's not what you... I... I can explain."

Faye looked from him to me, her painted-on eyebrows crinkling as she raised the natural ones beneath.

"Oh baby, you have got to be fucking kidding me," she said.

Trevor turned to face her. "No, I'm... I can explain."

A single hand snapped into the air and he fell silent as Faye turned to me, concern in her eyes. "Violet? That's your name?"

I nodded.

"Is he your boyfriend?"

I nodded again.

"And did you know he's into men?"

Again, I nodded. Faye pursed her lips almost hopefully.

"Did you know he had sex with me?"

I shook my head and the hopeful look on her face faded.

"Did he have permission to have sex with anyone *besides* you?"

There was no need to shake my head that time. Faye figured it out from the choked noise I made as tears sprung into my eyes.

TWO

TREVOR TRIED TO TELL me he'd slept with Faye—well, Rico, but she was Faye just then—so he could make some connections with other drag queens.

But all that did was piss Faye off even more.

Then he tried to tell Faye that I was crazy, which got her so upset that the other queens who were there promoting their drag show with her noticed. Suddenly I had a wall of gauzy fabric and feather boas and sequins surrounding me as Faye tore into Trevor.

Verbally, of course. Faye was the very definition of a pacifist. But you wouldn't have known it from the way Trevor started crying.

After they were done, Faye had taken me back to her place and let me cry as she peeled off layer after layer of Faye Laytio until a tall, slightly chubby Puerto Rican man named Rico was standing there, a few errant splotches of makeup still on his face as he gathered me in his arms.

"I'm sorry," he said. "So sorry. We're gonna get you out of there, okay?"

I sniffled, shaking my head. "I don't know anyone else here. I don't... don't even have a job."

Rico rubbed my back lightly. "You know me. I'll help you. Tomorrow, we'll go get your things and you can come stay here for a bit. We'll find you a job. And I'll…" He sighed, hugging me a bit tighter. "We both used condoms when I… when Trevor was here. But I'm guessing I'm not the only one he's done this with, so we should take you to get tested."

My laugh came out watery. "Oh, no, that's okay."

"*Chica*, you are talking to the wrong man if you think not getting tested is okay," he said stiffly. "You absolutely need to know if you caught something from that disgusting little—"

"No, I mean, I know I didn't," I said. "I… we never… did. It."

"Never at all? Not even… hands? Mouths?"

"No. I'm a… I'm still a virgin," I said, hoping Rico couldn't see that my face was red all the way up to my hairline.

"You never had sex, but you were *living* together?" he asked incredulously.

"Wait until you find out that I moved here illegally with him, too," I muttered, and Rico let go of me to clutch at his chest in a dramatic show of shock that made me giggle.

I don't know why Rico was so nice to me. I mean, I knew he felt bad that Trevor had cheated on me with him, but he went above and beyond. Not only did he let me move in with him, but apparently, he knew anyone and everyone in Vegas. That meant he could help me find a job that wouldn't look too closely at my whole "lack of a work visa and SIN card" thing while I tried to sort out what I was supposed to do to… well, you know.

Stay in Vegas.

He offered to help me get home instead, but home wasn't an option anymore. So Rico kindly called up a bar owner he knew named Dante and asked if he had any work available.

And sure, Dante was the kind of sleazy bar owner who was probably swaddled in red flags as a baby rather than knit blankets. But he paid under the table and had just opened a new bar, a place he creatively called

7

Dante's Bar. It was located in the cluster that was the Grand Bazaar Shops outside of Bally's, a collection of businesses that were kind of like an outdoor market had a baby with a strip mall.

I'd been nervous at first, working so boldly and so illegally right out in the open like that, but I'd realized quickly that no one cared. And if they had, Dante would have paid them not to. That still would have been cheaper for Dante than hiring someone legally, and as a sleazy bar owner, he was well versed in cutting every corner he could to save money.

Like hiring an illegal Canadian who had no bartending experience to work at a bar that sold expensive, shitty alcohol to tourists who lapped it up like they were lost in the desert and it was water from the Fountain of Youth.

And Dante's Bar did reasonably well, even though there was almost no *actual* draw to bring people into the bar. I had steadfastly refused to dress "sexier" despite the number of times Dante told me I should tie my t-shirt into a crop top or wear jean shorts that weren't so much jorts as they were janties. And I still sucked at bartending. And I was pretty sure he was cutting all the alcohol with water when it got delivered.

But it was on the Strip, so it made money. And more important-ly, directly across from Dante's Bar was a much better—and much *busier*—bar called Fit and Flair. There was often a lineup to get in, so people would come over to Dante's Bar to wait for a spot to open up before going over to Fit and Flair.

Which is where I'd seen *him*.

He embodied the bar name. *Fit* was barely a good enough word to describe how gorgeous he was. It didn't take into account his thick, dark hair or his high cheekbones and strong nose.

Or the neatly trimmed facial hair that was a little too long to be called stubble, but too short to truly be a beard.

Or his eyes, which were bright and lively and chocolatey brown.

Or his skin, which was a warm, tanned white.

Not even his hands, which were large and had gripped the bottles and shakers expertly as he put the *flair* into Fit and Flair.

I'd spent most of the night watching with my lips parted, staring through the glass walls between our two bars as he juggled bottles and threw ice and spun glasses on his hand with a bright, heart-melting smile on his face. Every few minutes, a cheer would float through the open doors, laughter and applause as he served up drink after drink. I didn't know if it was his first night—I'd been off the day before—but I was obsessed.

Despite the whole *thing* about his name.

THREE

"THE THING ABOUT HIS name is what?" Rico asked as he worked his fingers through my hair. "Is his name Trevor?"

He paused, then gasped.

"Or is he named *Rico* and you're worried you'll think of me when Mr. Dreamy takes you to Pound Town?"

I burst out laughing. "I don't know it."

"Wait, you don't know your co-worker's name?"

"He's not my co-worker. He works at Fit and Flair."

"Dante's still too cheap to hire someone so you're not working all by yourself late at night?"

"It's fine. It's not like I'm alone."

"You're literally working alone."

I rolled my eyes. "And I'm surrounded by other bars and businesses with people who are working just as late as me. I'm fine, *papi*."

He snorted back a laugh at my very Canadian and not at all Puerto Rican accent, then toyed with my hair affectionately. "Fine. You spent all night staring at the new guy at the bar across from yours and didn't even go over to introduce yourself?"

"Why would I? It's not like he even noticed me."

Rico sighed. "You have to give him a chance to notice you. By doing things like going over and introducing yourself."

"He seemed busy."

"Yeah, because he works at Fit and Flair, not at Dante's Dive. So if you want this man to peel the seal off your Pringles can—"

"Oh my *God*," I groaned. "Can we not refer to my vagina as a Pringles can? Or losing my virginity as *peeling* something?!"

"Fine. If you want this man to impale his bubble tea straw through the plastic lid of your vagina, then—"

"You're awful. The actual worst."

"You love it."

I tried not to smile, but it was true. "I don't know if I want... that."

Rico hummed. "With him, or at all?"

Sighing, I begrudgingly pulled myself off his lap. "It's not like I'm looking for a forever thing or even a more-than-one-night thing. It's just that after being with Trevor, I want to make sure my first time is with someone who... you know. Actually *wants* me. And doesn't think I'm weird for still being a virgin. And doesn't see it as some sort of achievement to fuck a virgin." Shrugging, I tapped my fingers along my denim-clad thigh. "And I just haven't met anyone like that yet."

"And you won't," Rico said. "Not unless you go up and introduce yourself to your mystery bartender."

"I don't even know him!"

"Exactly, which is why you have to introduce yourself." He put his arm around my shoulder. "You just go up to him and say, 'Hello, Mr. Dreamy. I work at Dante's across the way and my panties couldn't help but notice that your manly bits would fit exceptionally well into my girly bits and—'"

"Rico!" I said, dissolving into laughter.

"Okay, okay, what about you go up and ask for his name, and he tells you, and then he asks what your name is, and you say 'I'm named after a colour. If you guess it right, I'll give you fellatio. And if you guess it wrong, I'll introduce you to my friend, Faye Laytio—"

"*Rico!*"

"—when you take me out on a date to her next drag show,'" he finished. "And then tell him I like to be tipped in twenties."

He would have kept teasing me, and I would have kept letting him, but his phone went off a few minutes later with the booty call he'd been hoping for and I shooed him away to get ready so I could go to bed. Working until three a.m. had taken some getting used to, but now that I was, I kind of liked it, even if Rico fretted about me being at the bar alone so late. Most nights, I'd finish up and if Rico was performing, I'd pick him up from whatever club he was at first. We'd chat for a while, then I'd head to bed and wake up around noon the next day. Before going back to work, I'd have most of the day to run errands or hang out by the apartment complex's pool or visit with the new friends I'd made after Rico came into my life.

That night, though, I couldn't sleep. Even after Rico was long gone and I was tucked into bed alongside the clothing racks full of bejeweled gowns—the cost for my discounted rent being that half of the second bedroom remained Rico's drag closet—I lay awake. A beam of light from the streetlamps outside my window filtered through the blinds, making the sequins glitter like stars as I stared up at the ceiling.

I might have told Rico I didn't know if I wanted the man from Fit and Flair to... what was it, pop my Pringles lid? Whatever. And that was mostly true. I didn't know if he'd be the kind of guy I'd want to sleep with. Not to mention that he was absolutely beautiful from his head to at least his ankles—since I hadn't actually seen his toes—and I was...

like, not ugly, but not... not the kind of girl I imagined someone like him would be with.

I mean, I was okay. Pretty, even. There were certainly times that I didn't like my hair or my freckles, but show me someone who says they don't dislike *something* about their body sometimes and I'll show you a liar. But there were plenty of pretty things about me. Like my eyes. And my skin, pale as it may be even though I lived in a literal desert. As a redhead, SPF 50 was my best friend. And I liked my curves, even though sometimes I wished I was on the more petite and delicate side.

Especially when I pictured *him*.

Because that was the type of girl I pictured him with. One who got her hair done and wore makeup and knew how to dress to make herself look irresistible to anyone. One who was lithe but athletic, so she could plaster on those leggings that promised to make everyone's ass look good but really only made certain types of asses look good. A girl who could keep up with him at the gym or hiking or whatever he did to keep his body looking like that. Then he could use those big muscles of his to guide her every movement, to caress her body as he held her in his arms and made her *his*.

I couldn't picture myself in bed with him. I mean, I *could*—and, as my hand slid beneath the waistband of my sleep shorts, as I *did*—but not in a way that felt real. I could picture what those big hands would look like cupping my breasts or sliding up and down my sides, and I could almost feel his fingers instead of mine pushing between my folds as he played with my pussy, but at the same time, it was like it wasn't *me*.

Unattainable. Everything about him felt unattainable. But, to be fair, that was all due to a picture I'd created of him in my head. I didn't know his name, or his type, or if he was a sweetheart or a total asshole. And unless I introduced myself, I'd never know.

So, I thought, my hand between my legs as I wondered what his lips would feel like on my neck, maybe it was time to grow up a bit and just find out.

Maybe I'd go into work a little early and stop by so I could introduce myself.

Maybe I'd just see what happens.

FOUR

"His name is Jonah," I announced proudly.

Rico jolted up from his spot on the couch. He fumbled with the remote as the killer in the late-night horror movie he was watching began slashing at one of the unfortunate teenagers on screen. Moments later, with the teen in the middle of a yowling scream, Rico hit pause.

"Oh my God, Violet!" he gasped. "First of all, don't sneak up like that. You fucking terrified me—"

"Sorry. I thought you heard the door open." Frowning, I looked at the TV. "And why are you watching a horror movie? You hate horror."

"Clark recommended it and I—"

"Clark?"

Rico's cheeks darkened slightly. "You know Clark. He does drag as Vanessa Messa."

I couldn't hide the delight on my face. "Why are you so into watching a movie that Clark recommended?"

"Because he said it was interesting, and that's not the point. Don't you distract me because second, *finally*!" He heaved a dramatic sigh. "I can't believe it took you two weeks to introduce yourself."

I cleared my throat. "Well, um, I didn't, actually."

Rico lifted one eyebrow. "What?"

"But I found out his name!" I continued brightly. "And that's a step, right?"

"*How* did you find out his name?"

"Um..."

"Did you ask for it? Get close enough to him to read a nametag?" He folded one leg over the other. "Bump into him at Starbucks and start chatting because you vaguely recognized each other but before you could tell him your name, the barista called out his order and you overheard her?"

"Well... no."

"So?"

I hesitated, then sighed before collapsing on the couch beside him. "Two women who came in to wait for a spot at Fit and Flair asked me how I got anything done working across from Jonah all day and when I asked 'who's Jonah' they looked at each other and then burst out laughing and asked me what I knew about Scrabble tiles."

"... what?"

"That's what I said."

Rico looked bewildered, then shrugged before patting his lap twice and lifting his arms so I could lie down. "How did you know they meant him, then?"

"They pointed him out," I said as I settled my head against his leg so he could untangle my hair.

"Hmm. *Jonah*," Rico said slowly, rolling the name around his mouth as he loosened the hair ties at the end of my braids. "It's a sexy enough name to moan. *If* one were to grow some lady balls and do more than just nod towards him one of these days."

I could feel my cheeks turning red. Rico wasn't wrong, but I didn't know if I could ever bring myself to talk to Jonah first. It had taken a week before I'd even interacted with him by way of an acknowledging nod through the glass walls of our bars.

And the only reason *that* had happened was because I was trying to explain to a group of women who were part of a bachelorette party that Dante's was not associated with Fit and Flair. As such, I couldn't just "make him come over here" to serve them drinks. Flustered, I'd gestured pointedly towards Fit and Flair, and apparently my pointing had been so pointed that it caught Jonah's attention. He'd glanced up, those dark eyes of his so intense I could see them from across the walkway between the shops. Then he looked at the women around me and his perfectly shaped lips spread into a knowing smile. He jerked his chiselled jaw up, motioning towards me with his chin as if to tell me to send the women over to Fit and Flair.

At least, I hope that was what the head-jerk meant, because that's what I did after nodding thankfully at him and kicking the women out of my bar.

Since then, we'd exchanged nods a total of six times. On Friday, he saw me rush out of the bar after a patron forgot his wallet on the table. As I turned back to Dante's, he caught my eye, and another one of those half-smiles brightened his gorgeous face. Flustered and with my breath caught in my throat, I did the only thing I could think of, which was to nod in acknowledgement before scurrying back behind the bar.

Saturday, he must have taken a break or something, because he walked by the bar and glanced in while I was fighting with a group of men who insisted there wasn't any rum in their rum-and-cokes, even though they watched me pour a shot into each of them. As I was mentally reminding myself to tell Dante he'd started cutting the hard liquor too much, Jonah's eyebrow flicked up. Like he was some kind of Greek god sent to protect me from the horde of already-too-drunk guys hassling me, he mouthed something that kind of looked like "You okay?"

Or that's what I thought he mouthed. If it wasn't, he was probably confused by me nodding before I ducked behind the bar because my cheeks were as red as my hair.

On Sunday, we'd nodded to each other *twice*: once when I finally had enough of a lull to slide the doors shut so I could rush to the bathroom, and again when he was leaving for the night.

Though, he was being followed by a trail of women at the time and it was two a.m., so it might not have been a nod so much as a glance over his shoulder to see if they were still tailing him. Even still, he was swathed in streetlights and the heat of the night air, the shadows cast across his face morphing him into something ethereal and mythical and *phenomenal*.

Then I hadn't seen him for a few days. I worked eight to three every day except Tuesday and the occasional Wednesday, but his schedule was more varied and he seemed to start his shifts at six or seven and left around two.

Which brought us to today, when he'd nodded at me twice again, and the second time, he'd even flashed a bright, charming smile in my direction. I couldn't say it was at *me*, since he might have just been laughing because I'd spilled an entire bag of ice over the bar, but he smiled nevertheless. And some people might have thought that meant he was interested, but even if I'd been able to muster up my lady balls enough to approach him without two glass walls and a sidewalk between us, I couldn't have.

For one, there was the whole shifts-not-aligning thing. So unless I started going in early and made it far too obvious that I was doing it so I could see him, or going to Fit and Flair on his days off which was a gamble, since I didn't know *which* days those would be, an inadvertent opportunity to casually introduce myself after work wasn't going to happen.

What was more, though, was how busy the bar was.

Fit and Flair had always been popular, but since he'd started, it seemed busier than ever, especially with groups of women. I couldn't exactly blame them—he was like if a fairy-tale prince came to life and then took up CrossFit or whatever it was that guys like him did to stay ripped.

Because he was. He wouldn't have looked out-of-place standing on a pedestal at Caesars Palace, dressed in traditional Roman garb. Not that he wore shorts short enough for me to see his thighs, but he just looked like he'd have those big, meaty thighs that could pin a girl down. And his arms... he could have probably even held up someone as tall and curvy as me when I swooned into them.

So there were hordes of women trying to get into Fit and Flair. Dante wasn't complaining about that at all, since we were the lacklustre second choice for the disappointed guests who couldn't get a table right away. And I shouldn't have complained either, since most of the guests weren't disappointed enough to not leave a tip, so I was making more money, too. But even when I had a lull, Fit and Flair was bustling to fill orders and flip bottles, enthusiastic cheers constantly erupting from tourists lining the bar. So trying to walk in and introduce myself when they were busy like that would just be... I don't know.

Rude, I guess.

And then there was the hopelessness of even standing out enough for Jonah to remember me. I mean, it wasn't like he'd introduced himself to me. And it hadn't gone unnoticed that—well, okay, it *had* gone unnoticed until Dante skeevily pointed out in far less respectful terms that most of Fit and Flair's business was coming from the aforementioned groups of women. So when it came right down to it, Jonah probably could have gone home with a different woman or five every single night. And those women were all dressed for a night out on the Strip, in slinky dresses and high heels and low-cut tops.

Meanwhile, there I was in jean shorts that weren't even that short and a t-shirt that was just a fucking t-shirt.

"Is sexy Scrabble a thing?" I asked suddenly.

Rico's fingers stilled in my hair, then he hooted. "*What*?!"

I couldn't help but laugh along with him. "I mean, with the increase in women and now this Scrabble thing... maybe he's a hot Scrabble player? And these are all Scrabble fangirls who—"

Rico's laughter was so exuberant that I nearly fell off his lap on account of the way he started jostling his legs.

"Violet, baby," he giggled. "There's no *way*... I mean, I see your line of thought but—"

And then he dissolved into laughter again.

"I don't know what else it could be," I said when he'd calmed down enough to wipe the tears of laughter off his face. "I mean, I guess he could be heir to the Scrabble family fortune or something, maybe."

An errant chuckle made my head bounce again and Rico groaned. "*Chica*, no more. I worked my core way too hard at the gym for you to be this funny."

I smiled. "Sorry. I just wish I could find out."

He hummed, then began untangling my braids. "I have an idea of how you can find out what Jonah has to do with Scrabble."

I brightened. "Really?"

"Mm-hmm. It's a little out there, but stick with me, okay?"

"Okay."

"First, you go to work."

"Right."

"Then—and this is the key here, okay? Are you ready?"

Trying not to giggle, I nodded. "Yeah, I'm ready."

"Okay. It's an old Diaz family secret, but I think it's what you need." He leaned forward, his head over mine as he looked at me with wide, serious eyes. "You go to work, and then you *just fucking introduce yourself to him already!*"

FIVE

I DIDN'T INTRODUCE MYSELF to him.

The next day was Friday, which was always insanely busy. Worse, however, was that Jonah wasn't working that day. That was a complete downer on its own, since sneaking glances at him through the glass walls seemed to make the night go by faster. But it was made worse because all the Scrabble fans Jonah seemed to attract were *particularly* devastated that he wasn't there.

"Can you tell us when his next shift is?" the leader of one group of semi-drunk women asked as she paid for the margarita I'd just made her.

"No," I replied. "I don't know when he works."

"Can't you just check the schedule?"

I stared at her. "I... don't work there. I work here."

She looked at me snidely. "They're not the same business?"

"Um, no."

Huffing, she took a sip of her margarita, wrinkled her nose, then turned on her heel and walked away without tipping.

I'm sure the guys at Fit and Flair had their share of whiny bachelorettes and birthday girls, but they had the benefit of being on par or just slightly below Jonah's level of unattainable hotness. So the majority of their customers were still smiling and cheering as they watched the other bartenders pour towers of shots and plunk lit sparklers into slushy blue drinks.

I, unfortunately, was the wrong gender of broad-shouldered ginger for most of the patrons who *couldn't* get a seat at Fit and Flair. As such, my tips that night were abysmal. I tried to be upbeat and cheerful, but by the time three a.m. rolled around, I was exhausted, annoyed, and wanted nothing more than to get Rico from the club where he was performing and go home.

So of course, Rico wasn't ready to go when I got there.

Here, I texted as soon as I parked, leaving the car running while I waited.

And waited.

And waited.

Rico? I texted after ten minutes went by and he hadn't responded. I looked around, wondering if I'd missed him walking out, but that was unlikely. Rico didn't take his drag off until we got home and it was pretty hard to miss a six-foot-something drag queen dripping in rhinestones and feathers. *Are you almost ready?*

Another five minutes went by without an answer, and then another five. Sighing, I sent one last text—*Parking and coming to find you*—and pulled out of the rideshare lane, not sure if I was more annoyed or worried.

Once I'd parked, pleaded with the bouncer to let me in without charging me cover because I was just trying to find my friend and it would only take two minutes since, again, she was a six-foot-something bedazzled drag queen, then begrudgingly paid said cover when that didn't work, I decided I was annoyed.

Especially when I took three steps into the club and saw Rico—well, Faye Laytio—on the dance floor surrounded by a throng of women with bleached blonde hair and low-cut shirts showing off what I was pretty sure were mostly silicone breasts.

I usually loved seeing my friend in her element, entertaining people and spreading joy as she shook her padded hips from side to side and taught a slightly-too-inebriated girl to cha-cha. But that night, I was annoyed she hadn't texted me so I could just go home and sleep after my awful shift.

As pulsating blue lights flashed to the beat of the music playing, I slipped past a group of loud people who were talking about guys on the Eiffel Tower and narrowly avoided bumping into a woman grinding between two men who were significantly shorter than her. Just before I reached the group of women dancing with Faye, she turned. Since I was wearing a black t-shirt and denim Bermuda shorts and stuck out like a sore thumb amidst the other patrons clad in short dresses and heels so high that some of them were almost the same height as me, she noticed me immediately.

"*Violet!*" she said loudly, a grin on her face, then widened her arms as she gestured at the people around her. "Ladies, meet my beautiful bestie and roommate extraordinaire!"

"Violet!" they shouted drunkenly, and the one closest to me threw an arm over my shoulder.

"First time at the conference, sweetie?" she asked kindly.

"Oh, she's not here for that," Faye said with a loud laugh. "She's here to pick me up because I am a horrendously irresponsible person who didn't realize it was that time already since I was having *so* much fun with you!"

The women laughed and I looked up at Faye with confusion. "What conference?"

"Nothing, *chica*." She shook one of the women off her gently and leaned down, lowering her voice to a conspiratorial shout-whisper. "You won't *believe* how much I've made tonight. I had no idea that... well, I'll tell you when we get home. C'mon, I'll get you a spot at the bar to chill in for a while. Give me another half an hour and—"

"I've already been waiting for twenty minutes," I said as evenly as I could.

Faye grinned cheekily. "So another thirty isn't that bad, right?"

I didn't smile back and the corners of her heavily painted mouth flicked down.

"Violet—"

"I want to go home," I said. "I've had an awful night. It was busy and everyone was yelling at me because Jonah wasn't at Fit and Flair, which means I also didn't get to *see* him and I'm just *done.*"

She looked like she was about to protest, but the fact that I was about to burst into tears on the dance floor of a crowded club stopped her.

"I'm sorry, Vi. I am. You go. I'll crash with Vanessa Messa tonight. And I'll make you a big batch of chouquettes on my next day off to make up for being a forgetful old hag, okay?"

I probably looked like a child as I pursed my lips into a pouty frown, but I did love it when she baked pastries. Nodding stiffly, I let Faye press a loud kiss to my temple before she patted me on the back.

"I'll see you at home sometime, then," I said.

"Love you, *chica,*" she said, and then disappeared in a whirl of sparkles and sequins as she went back to continue partying.

With another sigh, I turned, weaving my way through the people dancing and shouting conversations at each other. All was fine until I reached the edge of the dance floor and a particularly exuberant person threw their arm out, almost smacking me across my face. I dodged out of the way without them hitting me but unfortunately, the hand they'd thrown out was holding a plastic cup. A slosh of liquid splattered out of the cup and onto the dance floor, which wasn't quite sticky enough to stop me from sliding through the puddle.

"Oh, *fu*—" I gasped as I stumbled, but before I fell, an arm slipped around my waist and caught me.

"Whoa there," said the owner of said arm, which when I looked up, turned out to be a skinny white man with a thin, drawn face and glazed eyes that reflected the pulsating blue lights of the bar. "You okay or—wow."

"I'm okay," I said unsteadily.

He didn't let go of my waist, just stared at me.

"Thank you," I continued. "I was going home."

"Already?" he asked, his breath reeking of what was either cheap tequila or rubbing alcohol. "But I just caught you, baby."

I looked out of the corner of my eye towards the dance floor, but I couldn't see Faye from where I was. "I'd like to leave, please."

"One drink. To thank me for graciously making sure you didn't fall."

"No, I'm—"

He pulled me a bit closer and without thinking, I reached up, put both hands on his chest, and pushed. He didn't so much as budge, but he did glance down at my hands on his chest before looking back up at me with a raised eyebrow.

"Rude," he said in a terrifyingly low voice.

"Let me go," I said.

"Or what?"

The lighting in the club changed just then. So did the music, probably, but I couldn't have said what it sounded like as warm reds and oranges filled the space and a large hand clamped down on the skinny man's shoulder. My eyes followed that hand to a muscular arm with familiar tattoos peeking out beneath a tight t-shirt, then up even further to a set of wide shoulders, a chin of scruffy stubble, and rich brown eyes.

"'Sup, Ginger Girl," Jonah said.

I'd never heard him speak before. His voice was deep, a rich baritone that made my heart stutter. Behind him, the club lights shifted and changed, throwing a golden glow across his dark hair like he was some kind of saviour there to protect me. For a moment after seeing him, I forgot everything from my own name to how words worked.

Unfortunately for everyone involved, I eventually remembered the latter.

"Hey, Scrabble Guy," I said, my voice high-pitched.

I wasn't sure what was funnier: the way the skinny man's face went pale, or the wide-eyed shock on Jonah's face as I called him *Scrabble Guy* instead of literally anything else.

Well, funny in hindsight. At the time, my stomach dropped as Jonah's lips parted, but no words came out. He stared at me for a moment with a blank look on his face, but before I could panic too much, it morphed into amusement and his hand squeezed the skinny man's shoulder harder.

"You okay?" he asked me.

"I'm trying to leave," I replied.

Jonah looked at the skinny man. "Let go, Kyler."

The man did. As soon as his arm went slack and before anyone could say anything else, I turned on my heel and beelined for the exit.

SIX

As MUCH AS I was dying to tell Rico about Jonah stepping in to help me at the club that night, I didn't.

Even though he'd said he would crash at Vanessa Messa's house that night, I'd expected to see him before I had to go back to work the next night. But he and Vanessa—a.k.a. Clark—had finally realized they were perfect for each other, so he just... didn't come home. I was, of course, ecstatic for them and Rico was on cloud nine, so we spent our short text exchange early that afternoon talking about what had happened.

And we also have the same size feet, Rico said in his text. *So this doubles my stiletto collection!*

Then, before I could type a reply, he messaged again.

Sorry, chica, talk later. Clark just got out of the shower and is walking around shirtless looking for his glasses. I need to take full advantage of this.

So I didn't tell him then about running into Jonah. I thought I would have time to tell him before I went to work, since he would have to come home to get into drag for his performance that night, but it wasn't too long after that when Dante messaged me.

Need you to come in asap. Callie ate a bad hot dog on break and got the squirts. She can't stay till the end of her shift.

I wrinkled my nose before texting him back. *So I'm working an 11 hour shift by myself on a Saturday?*

I don't have time to fight with you on this. Cover the end of Callie's shift and you can have tomorrow night off.

I didn't even hesitate before accepting that deal. Sure, a night off meant one less night's worth of tips, but Sunday nights were dead anyway and, as broke as I felt most of the time, one shift wasn't going to ruin me completely.

Callie was long gone by the time I got there, so the bar was closed and locked up. Dante was probably livid about it, but I got there before things picked up for the evening, so it wasn't too bad. As I unlocked the door and dragged the sandwich board advertising the two-for-one happy hour special that was usually long done by the time I started, I glanced over at Fit and Flair. There were three guys working, but none of them were Jonah. I bit my lip, hoping that he had just gotten lucky and they'd given him a weekend off. That was far better than the other option, which was that he either got fired or quit.

Before I could worry about it too much, though, a couple in their thirties wandered up, saw the happy hour sign, and decided they needed a pair of horribly mixed Bloody Marys.

Things were steady from then on. It wasn't like the evening shift where I was so busy I could barely breathe sometimes, but people came in at a steady pace. Apparently, it didn't matter to people how shitty the alcohol was or how bad I was at making drinks, so long as those shitty drinks were half their usual cost.

So it was busy enough that I was hustling back and forth across the bar, not really paying attention to what was happening around me. Then happy hour ended just as the evening rush began and I was hustling even harder.

Maybe if I hadn't been so busy, I would have noticed a few things.

Like that Fit and Flair was even busier than Dante's was with their now-typical crowd of mostly women.

Or that there were a handful of men in my bar that were grumbling about their wives taking their sweet ass time.

And maybe, if I'd been less focused on making a line of Jägerbombs for someone's twenty-first birthday, I would have noticed that people weren't asking me about Fit and Flair as much as they usually did.

And that no one was complaining about Jonah not being there.

And that Trevor had walked into my bar.

In fairness, Trevor didn't notice me either. That was because I was facing the other direction, making sure I didn't spill as I poured six shots. It wasn't until I turned around that my ex-boyfriend realized the braided red hair he'd been staring at belonged to the girl he'd moved to Vegas with and subsequently cheated on.

Unfortunately, he realized it at the exact same moment that I realized my cheater of an ex-boyfriend was sitting on a stool at my bar, his mouth hanging open as the blood drained from his face. I froze in place, staring at him to the soundtrack of the six people behind me cheersing the birthday girl and pounding back their Jägerbombs.

The last time I'd seen him had been the day after I found out he was cheating. Rico had called up a few of his friends who had been there the night before and they all came with me to the small apartment Trevor and I had shared so I didn't have to pack my things by myself. Trevor had hovered as we packed, muttering now and again when someone tried to take something that was arguably his, then pleading with me using his eyes whenever that someone would turn to me and loudly ask if it was something I wanted to take.

Most of the time, I said no, he could keep it. But I did take his favourite coffee mug. And my hair straightener, even though he used it for his wigs all the time and I never used it.

Even then, when I'd been devastated and terrified and felt completely lost, I'd been a bit vindictive. Not *very* vindictive, since I was panicking about things like being homeless or getting deported, but I'd still been resentful about how Trevor had played me.

Now? Now I was bitter.

"What are you doing here?" he finally asked.

I blinked, then glanced down at the bottle of Jägermeister still in my hand before looking back up at him.

"I work here," said a voice that sort of sounded like mine but was full of derision and repulsion.

"Right," he said. "But—"

"What are *you* doing here?" I asked.

The disgust in my voice seemed to unsettle him and he glanced at an older man with thick salt-and-pepper hair sitting beside him.

"We were going for a drink next door, but it's too busy," he said.

"Well, that sucks." I gestured towards the door. "Get out."

"What?" said the man next to him.

"Get out," I repeated, glaring at the man. "Leave. Bye-bye. Too-dle-oo." I waved my hand erratically. "Why would you even want to be here? Vamoose."

"Vi, wait," Trevor said softly. "Are you doing okay?"

"Excuse me?"

There was a pained look on his face. "I just... I didn't even know you were still in town. And now I see you here, working at a..." His nose wrinkled slightly as he glanced around. "I mean, kind of a dive bar? I know what happened with us was rough, but I just... I want you to be okay."

"What happened with us?" I repeated. "You mean when you cheated on me after I moved with you to an entirely different country to support your dream, knowing that I wouldn't be able to go home? Or are you saying it like that because your new friend here doesn't know about it?"

His face turned red. "Yes, that's what I mean. And no, Grant... knows."

The other man—Grant—put a hand on Trevor's shoulder.

"Well, good for you for owning up to being a cheating asshole," I said.

He sighed. "Look, is there anything I can do to... you know. Help you?"

"Help me?" I snorted. "*Help* me? What do you think I need help with?"

"Well—"

"I'm doing *great*," I continued. "Like, better than *ever*."

And that was true. I was doing great, aside from the working illegally and potential-to-be-deported thing.

And I should have shut my mouth right then and not said another word unless it included something like "Get the fuck out of my bar right now."

I should have insisted they walk away and gone on with my night as I usually did.

But I didn't.

"I'm doing so good. It's crazy," I continued. "Like, my roommate and I have this super amazing apartment with an amazing view. Are you still living in that crappy apartment we had when we first moved here? I can't even imagine living somewhere without a pool anymore. And I have a steady job and I get paid really well here, obviously."

"Right," Trevor said in a tone that was full of condescendingly sympathetic disbelief.

I saw red.

"And it's surprising you say you're doing so good," I continued. "Because a bunch of *my* friends do drag and none of them have mentioned seeing you around anywhere."

"That would be because I'm not living here anymore." Trevor reached over and put his hand on Grant's leg. "I moved to Los Angeles after my boyfriend and I met. We're just back for a... um... conference."

"Oh," I said, and that's when I *really* should have shut my mouth. Like, even as I opened my mouth, I knew I should shut my mouth.

And yet...

"Well, my boyfriend and I talked about moving one day, but right now we love being in Vegas," I said.

Trevor looked stunned. "You have a boyfriend?"

I glared at him. "Of course I have a boyfriend. Why *wouldn't* I have a boyfriend?"

"I just—"

"What? You thought I wouldn't be able to do better than you?"

"No, I—"

"Well, I *have* done better than you. A lot better. He's hotter and smarter and not a cheater like you are and he actually likes me instead of just using me," I said.

"That's great, Vi," he said earnestly. "I'm happy for you. I really am. What's his name?"

"I—what?" I asked.

Thank God he had said he was happy for me. Both he and Grant seemed to assume that I was stunned rather than floundering desperately in the lie I had made up for absolutely no reason.

"I'm happy for you," he repeated. "I am *seriously* sorry for what I did to you, Vi. I was in a bad place when we came here and I'm trying to do better now. That doesn't excuse it but... but I'm glad you're doing well."

"Oh," I said. "Um. Thanks."

An awkward moment passed before Trevor raised his eyebrows expectantly. "So...?"

My instinct was to say Rico because Rico was my best friend and would have absolutely pretended to be my boyfriend if necessary. Luckily, I stopped myself in time, since Trevor would have seen right through that on account of the whole "cheating on me with Rico" thing. So after hesitating a moment longer, I said the only other name I could think of.

"Jonah."

SEVEN

It should have been fine.

I mean, theoretically, I could have said *any* name. Bob. Horatio. Hell, I could have said "Oh, funnily enough, his name is *also* Grant" and that would have been just coincidental enough to sound plausible.

So even though I was making this all up, it should have been one of those little lies that made me look better to my ex and would have zero consequences as soon as he walked away.

But as soon as I spoke, Grant and Trevor exchanged looks.

"Jonah?" Grant repeated. "The guy who works at the bar across from here?"

And what was I supposed to say to that? "Oh, no, it's a *different* hot guy named Jonah. You don't know him. He goes to another school. In Canada. And doesn't believe in social media or photography so I don't have a picture of him."

Like that wouldn't have been completely obvious.

So I just... nodded.

It was almost funny watching the thoughts flicker across Trevor's face. Stunned surprise and concern and slight disgust and—my personal favourite—an almost reflective self-consciousness before his cheeks started turning red.

"That's... lovely," Grant said flatly, glancing at Trevor.

"I... *really*?!" Trevor said, his whole face pink. "You... *you're* dating Jonah Arizona?"

Jonah Arizona? Yeesh What a name.

Trevor said it as if I should know who that was. And since I was claiming he was my boyfriend, I probably should have. But the name didn't stand out and I was already in this deep, so I put a haughty look on my face and folded my arms.

"Yes, Trevor, I am."

"You," he repeated, then frowned. "Are you sure about that?"

"Do you have some kind of *problem* with it?" I asked.

He studied me for a moment, then looked over at Fit and Flair. When he looked back at me, there was clear skepticism in his eyes.

"You just aren't the type," he said frankly. "I might have fucked things up, but I know how you are, Violet."

"Fuck you, Trevor," I said. "Get out of my bar."

"Gladly," Grant said before Trevor could respond. "It looks like a spot is available across the way. Shall we, pet?"

Trevor held my eye for another moment before sliding off his bar stool.

"Yeah," he said. "And don't worry, Vi. I'll tell your *boyfriend* you said hello."

Then they turned, striding out of Dante's Bar and towards the two open bar stools that had just opened up at Fit and Flair. I followed them with my eyes, which is when I finally noticed that Jonah was standing behind the bar, the bottom half of a martini shaker sitting sideways on his elbow.

Of course. I'd started early. He wouldn't have started before I did that day.

And now...

I wondered if I could get away with calling Dante and telling him I had food poisoning, too.

A swell of cheering came from Fit and Flair as Jonah tossed a bottle in the air, then caught it so he could balance it on top of the shaker. Just as it settled in place, he glanced towards me, his eyes catching mine. A sweet, lopsided smile spread on his face and he gave a subtle nod. When I didn't return it, he almost dropped the bottle and martini shaker, just barely catching both items before they hit the floor.

Though, that could have been because his eyes slid away from mine and noticed Trevor and Grant walking into the bar.

"Um, *excuse* me!" someone shouted behind me, snapping their fingers. "We've been waiting for a refill!"

"Oh, fuck off," I muttered.

"Excuse me?"

"I said sorry to put you off," I said, tearing my eyes off Jonah and turning around. "My apologies. I... you want more Jägerbombs? Six for the price of five for your wait?"

They cheered and I set to work, steadfastly trying not to look over at Fit and Flair. I succeeded until I was pouring the last shot of Jägermeister and felt that strange prickling sensation of someone watching me. Looking up, I saw Trevor and Grant both twisted on their bar stools as they looked towards me while Jonah stood behind the bar, staring in my direction with an unreadable expression on his face.

"Uh... I think you're spilling that," someone said, and I snapped my head back to see a puddle of Jägermeister spilling all over the bar.

Fuck.

EIGHT

THE ONLY THING THAT stopped me from dropping everything and putting as much distance as possible between me and Jonah, Trevor, and Grant was that Dante would likely be much more invested in tracking me down than the US Immigration office.

And probably much less lenient.

So cutting and running was not an option, not even when Jonah put down his martini shaker and said something to one of the other bartenders while I hurried to mop up the alcohol I'd spilled.

Not even when he stepped out from behind the bar at Fit and Flair and started towards the exit.

And even though my heart started pounding so hard that my hands were shaking and I was starting to feel lightheaded, there was nothing I could do as he crossed the walkway to Dante's and stepped through the entrance.

"Hey Ginger Girl," he called in a smooth, warm voice.

The noise of my bar faded to silence as heads turned and eyes widened at his voice. As I looked at him, hoping the wild panic coursing through me wasn't showing on my face, the noise returned, people turning away to make their surprise less obvious and hissed conversations to the tune of "Oh my *God*, that's *him*" filling the room.

"Heh," was the noise that came out of my mouth. It was high-pitched and I wasn't sure if it was supposed to be "Hey" or "Hi" or "Please just let me crawl under the bar and die of embarrassment in peace."

The corner of Jonah's mouth twitched. "Can I talk to you for a sec?"

Fuck.

Fuck, fuck, fuck.

Fuck.

I nodded, because what the hell else could I do, and put the Jägermeister-soaked bar towel down before wiping my liquor-dampened hands on my denim shorts. It took a moment, but I willed my feet to step out from behind the safety of the heavy wooden bar and past the tables of patrons watching out of the corner of their eyes. Jonah waited patiently and once I was close enough, I cleared my throat.

"Hey," I said as I walked up. "So, here's the th—"

And then he slipped his hand around my waist, pulled me forward, and kissed me.

For a second, I forgot how.

How to kiss.

How to breathe.

How to even think.

I stared at his eyelids, my mind blank, warm lips pressed to mine as he held my body against his. For another second, I wondered what the fuck was happening and fretted about the hushed gasps and murmurs around us and, strangely, if my breath still smelled like the ham sandwich I'd eaten for dinner or if the Coke I'd been sipping on since then had covered it.

But only for a second, because holy *fuck* could Jonah kiss.

I melted. There was no other way to describe it. One moment, I was certain I was going to die of humiliation, and the next I was a mess of lips and warm breaths and tingling electricity shooting up and down my body. My eyes closed of their own volition and somehow, my hands ended up resting on those thick, muscular shoulders of his. He held me close but not too tightly, just enough that our bodies brushed against each other and I felt like my entire soul was enrobed by him.

I'd never had someone kiss me like that. I'd never kissed someone and *felt* it, like his lips weren't just pressed to mine but were tracing every inch of my body. Like a clone of his mouth was sucking on my neck and tickling down my sternum and making something warm and achy pool deep in my core.

All while his mouth was just touching mine.

That was the kind of kiss that made impulsive, rash decisions. That made hands wander and clothes fall to the ground and breathless noises fill the air in a way I hadn't ever experienced.

That turned girls like me into absolute addicts, craving more, and more, and—

"Oh," I said as he pulled back.

The corners of Jonah's eyes crinkled. "Couldn't wait till later. How's work going, baby?"

"Uh-huh."

He held in a laugh, glancing to the side before lowering his voice so I could barely hear it. "Don't worry. I played along. Are you alright?"

"Right," I breathed. "Right, that... I'm sorry. I'm so sorry."

"It's okay."

"It's not. I don't even know you and I pretended you were my boyfriend and then my stupid cheating ex went over there and you—"

"Wait, your ex?" he asked, the amusement fading from his eyes. "Grant or the younger guy?"

"The... the younger one."

"And he cheated on you?"

I nodded.

"And he thought he could... Jesus fuck."

"I'm so sorry I dragged you into this. I just said the first name I could think of and—"

"I thought you thought my name was Scrabble Guy," he said.

My cheeks *burned*. "No, I just—"

"It's okay." Shaking his head, he brought a hand up to my cheek, his fingers caressing the heated skin tenderly and making all words disappear from my mind again. "Listen, I've got your back. I told him we're together and that you're cool with everything. I have to get back to work, but I'll stop by later, okay?"

Then he kissed me one more time and any of my remaining brain cells dissolved into the warm wetness that was making its way between my legs. When he pulled away and let go, it took everything in me not to collapse into a heap of arousal on the floor of the bar.

"See you after work, baby," he said as he turned to leave.

"Yeah," I said, then blinked twice. "Wait! Jonah, wait."

He stopped and looked at me, eyebrows raised.

"Violet," I said.

"Huh?"

"My, um... name," I said quietly. "It's Violet."

A sweet, seductive smile spread across his lips. "Good call. Probably should know my girlfriend's name isn't actually Ginger Girl."

With that, he walked back to Fit and Flair. After I tore my eyes away from the deliciously curved ass filling out his cargo shorts, I had a perfect view of the indignant anger written all over Trevor's face. Pressing my lips together, I tried not to laugh as I turned to walk back to my bar, where the girls from the birthday party were sitting silently with wide eyes.

"Sorry," I said as I went back behind the bar. "Did you need another drink?"

"Girl," said one of them, her voice awed. "You're dating *Scrabble Tiles*?!"

"Um..." I said. "Yes?"

The girls exchanged looks and then leaned in.

"You have to tell us what it's like," pleaded the birthday girl, who had a satin sash across her chest.

I frowned. "What?"

"Dating him. Oh my *God*," said a brunette with skin so tanned it was almost orange. "He's probably fabulous in bed."

I gaped at her, so shocked I couldn't say anything.

"Right?" said another girl, this one wearing a purple sequin tube top and probably some kind of miniskirt, though I couldn't see it over the edge of the bar. "Is he as good as he seems in his videos?"

"*Please* say yes," said a blonde girl, who then tilted her head back, almost moaning. "I swear, he's my hall pass."

The birthday girl burst out laughing. "What? *He's* your hall pass?"

"Of course! If I'm gonna fuck someone other than my boyfriend, I want it to be someone who like, knows what he's doing. And Jonah Arizona *knows* what he's doing." She turned to me with a devilish look on her face. "Right?"

"Frankly, I'm impressed you can even walk properly," said the girl in the purple tube top. "If someone blew my back out like that on the regular, I don't think I'd be able to stand up straight."

"Especially with a—" The birthday girl cackled and made a jerking-off motion with her hand. "—that big."

"I've always wondered if it's real," the brunette said, looking at me coyly. "Is he? As big as he looks in the videos?"

"Excuse me?" I said, shocked. "That's... you're talking about... my... my..."

WHAT HAPPENS IN VEGAS

"Yeah, assholes." The sixth girl, who had silky black hair, glared at her friends. "Just because he's a porn star doesn't mean you can ask her about their sex life. That's so *rude*."

A...

What?

A *what*?!

NINE

"Hey, Ginger Girl."

I nearly dropped the bottle of vodka I'd been refilling. Fumbling for a moment, I managed to catch it, then slammed it down on the bar as I looked up to see Jonah watching me with amusement.

"Sorry," he said. "I didn't mean to sneak up on you."

"It's okay," I said quickly. "I just wasn't expecting... anyone."

The bar was dead. It had been for nearly an hour at that point, which was pretty typical. We weren't one of the night clubs and once things began to slow down, any stragglers went to Fit and Flair instead of Dante's. It worked out well, since it meant I could get almost everything cleaned up and cashed out just a few minutes after three instead of having to stick around after we officially closed.

But more than that, I'd been lost in the same spiralling thoughts I'd been grappling with all night. The same thoughts I had each time I glanced surreptitiously at Fit and Flair and saw my fake boyfriend as he stood on a bar stool to pour a stream of liquor directly into the mouth of some girl lying on the bar. Or when I saw him toss cherries in the air and catch them with his teeth.

Jonah—the guy I was not-so-secretly obsessed with—did porn.

It wasn't that his job itself bothered me. Sex work was work. I might have been a somewhat naïve Canadian virgin, but I wasn't so fragile as to be dismayed by the concept of people using sex to make money. I wouldn't have lasted long in a place literally known as "Sin City" if I was so easily scandalized.

It was the whole "naïve virgin" part of the equation.

Jonah was so good at his job, women were literally tracking him down to where he worked as *not* a porn star to see him. He was so good at his job that people not only recognized him in public, but *acknowledged* that they recognized him, meaning they were outright admitting they watched porn. That might not have been completely unusual, but even in Vegas, that wasn't super typical.

And I was... me. In a different decade, I would've been one hell of a catch on account of the sturdy hips, broad shoulders, and virgin status. But that decade would have also been within a century that didn't have indoor plumbing or anything resembling women's rights.

Someone like Jonah wasn't going to have any sort of interest in me. Not like *that*. Not when he could be with people who were the literal embodiment of society's desires.

And who knew what they were doing.

And who didn't end up so turned on from just a *kiss* that they could barely function for the rest of their shift.

So no, him having sex for a living didn't upset me. It was just that it made him even more unattainable. I guess, despite my certainty that he was completely unattainable before I'd found it out, I *had* been holding out a bit of hope. Enough hope that when the shock of hearing Jonah was a porn star wore off and there was a lull in customers, I'd pulled out my phone to text Rico so I could get some sympathy.

But there was already a message from Rico telling me he wouldn't need a ride that night because it was the last night of the Indie Adult

Entertainers conference that was taking place at the hotel beside the club he and Clark were performing at, which was why he'd been late the night before.

So don't worry about picking me up, he finished. *Me and Clarkie are gonna go back to his place afterwards and have sex on the mountain of tips we make.*

Okay. Have fun, I replied. *By the way, Jonah does porn.*

Despite the fact that I knew Rico was supposed to begin his performance as Faye not five minutes later, he texted back immediately.

HE WHATTTTTTTTTTT

I saw him at the club last night before I left.

I could almost hear Rico roll his eyes in his response. *Just because he was at last night's afterparty doesn't mean he does porn, chica.*

I started typing a response, but another text came in before I finished.

NOT JONAH ARIZONA??????

Yes Jonah Arizona.

You're joking. Oh my god. Jonah Arizona was in this club last night and I didn't even notice?????

You know him?

Have you not SEEN his videos? Straight boys aren't my thing, but I'd make an exception for him. His solo work is— and then he inserted a chef's kiss emoji. *You should look him up.*

While I was still trying to process the fact that my roommate had seen my crush naked and likely gotten off to him, he texted again.

I would just like to clarify, after Miss Vanessa Messa reminded me that I am being a Messa-y bitch right now, that I would not ACTUALLY make an exception for him. Partly because Vanessa Messa don't share and mostly because I would not do that to you, chica. I forgot about that stupid asshole you used to date.

He had to go onstage then, so I didn't end up telling him that said stupid asshole ex-boyfriend had been here or about the real kiss with my new fake boyfriend who happened to be a porn star. Or that I was moping about all of it. Rico was busy and didn't need me bringing him down.

Instead, I tucked my phone into my pocket, steadfastly ignoring Rico's suggestion to look Jonah up. Not only was I fairly certain Jonah's work was not, in fact, safe for work, I was pretty sure I wouldn't be able to look at him anymore if I watched any of it. At all.

Not because I was embarrassed, but if his *kiss* made me feel like I was going to implode into a puddle of goo, I couldn't imagine trying to make eye contact after seeing him... well.

And if I couldn't make eye contact, I would have to look somewhere else when he talked to me, which was even worse because then I might not be able to keep my eyes off his—

And that was what I was still thinking about when Jonah walked into the bar and spooked me.

TEN

"BUSY NIGHT?" JONAH ASKED, sliding onto one of the bar stools.

"Steady," I replied. "Yours?"

Before he could answer, I cringed and shook my head.

"Stupid question. I could see you. Of course you were busy."

"So you were watching me, then?"

"I..."

Jonah chuckled. "I'm kidding, Ginger Girl."

Trying to laugh, I nodded. "What, um... are you doing here?" My face burned immediately. "I mean, do you want a drink or... or something?"

He smiled. "Well, I had to come and check on my fake girlfriend to make sure she was doing okay. But sure, I'll keep you company and have a drink. What's your specialty?"

"A can of beer."

He burst out laughing. "Don't want to dirty a glass?"

"No, I just suck at making drinks."

"I doubt that." He picked up the cocktail menu on the bar, which was just a stained piece of crumpled cardstock. "C'mon. Let me try your Sex on the Beach."

I bit my lip to hide an immature smile, but the pinkness of my cheeks gave me away. Jonah grinned as he put the cocktail menu back down.

"You're kinda weird, you know that?" he said as I turned to collect the glass and bottles I needed.

"How so?"

He shrugged. "Usually I'm pretty good at figuring out how people will react to things. But you? Like, on one hand, you're unexpectedly cool."

I couldn't bite back the smile that time. "That is definitely the best word to describe my coolness."

He looked sheepish. "That came out wrong. I just meant that like, when I kept seeing you around and you were just smiling or nodding at me, I thought you were someone who was uncomfortable with people who do what I do."

I looked up, horrified. "No, that wasn't at all—"

"It's okay," he said, flashing an easy, charming smile at me. "It's not a big deal. Some people are and that's their problem, not mine. Besides, then I saw you at the afterparty last night and figured maybe you just hadn't had a chance to say hi or something. But then today, you go from claiming I'm your boyfriend and kissing me to turning beet-red when I say the word 'sex.'"

I laughed awkwardly. "I... yeah."

"So you're kinda weird," he said, smiling kindly. "But like, intriguing weird. And I have to thank you."

I looked up from measuring the ingredients for his drink. "For what?"

"Being cool about it at all." He licked his lips and suddenly the air of self-assured confidence that usually surrounded him dissipated into something far more vulnerable. "When I started doing porn, I didn't expect how hard it would be to like... meet people. Outside of it, I mean. I knew some people would treat me differently and maybe it was naïve of me, but I didn't think it was going to define everything about me, you know? So like, for you to see me as more than just a guy who does porn and—"

He started laughing, shaking his head.

"—I mean, you called me 'Scrabble Guy' to my *face*. I know everyone does, but no one usually just calls it out like that. It was kinda refreshing."

Uh-oh. I felt my breath catch. "Well, um..."

"And then, like, today. Pretending I'm your boyfriend?" He held up his hands reassuringly. "Not that I'm trying to pressure you into dating me for real or hitting on you or anything, okay? But saying something like that without being embarrassed or ashamed, even if it was fake... it means a lot. So, thank you. For letting me see how unexpectedly and awesomely cool you are. Even if you get weird when people say 'sex.'"

And oh, I should have just let him think that. I *should* have. But the guilt was too much, and I felt myself wincing, sure my cheeks were going to be stained permanently red.

"Well, I think you're about to discover how expectedly awkward and moronic I am," I said.

He raised his eyebrows. "Oh?"

"Yeah." I sighed, looking back down at the ingredients in front of me. "I didn't... know. That you... What you do. Until after you... after we kissed."

"Wait, really?" he said.

Wincing, I poured a shot of schnapps into the glass. "Yeah. I don't watch much porn and I didn't know you were... you know."

"But... last night... you were at the party."

"I didn't know there was a party," I said. "I was there to pick my roommate up, but he didn't want to leave yet."

"Oh," he said, his face brightening. "But your roommate's in the industry?"

"Well... no. He was performing at the club. He does drag."

"Oh." His voice went quiet again. "Which queen?"

"Faye Laytio? She's Puerto Rican and about six-and-a-half feet tall."

He nodded. "Yeah. Bright orange outfit. She was really good. So then today... Grant told you?"

"What?" I said, looking up.

"Grant. Guy who was with your ex?" He gestured towards Fit and Flair. "He told you what I do?"

"No. Why would he—" I stopped, thinking. Trevor had looked shocked, but he'd asked if I was *really* dating Jonah Arizona.

Which meant he absolutely knew who Jonah Arizona was and what he did for a living.

And he and his boyfriend were specifically *looking* for Jonah Arizona.

"Grant's a—" Jonah made heavily exaggerated air quotes on either side of his head. "—'talent agent' with one of the big studios. They've been trying to get me to sign on with them for a while now. Though, I'd be surprised if they tried again after what I said to him tonight."

"I'm sorry."

"Why? I don't want to work for them." He sighed. "Well, in any case. Sorry you got tangled up in that."

"Me? I'm sorry *you* got tangled up in that." I poured orange juice into the drink. "I shouldn't have lied to him at all, but it made me so *mad* that he was here with his boyfriend after everything he did. And anyway—" I laughed, shaking my head "—that explains the look on their faces when I said you were my boyfriend. Trevor looked like he was rethinking every decision he's ever made, and isn't that the best revenge?"

"Dating a porn star? Sure."

I looked up from his drink, frowning. "I meant dating someone they wanted something from so I had the distinct pleasure of watching him realize he wasn't going to get it."

Jonah wasn't looking at me, but a small smile crossed his lips. I put a straw in his drink and slid it towards him.

"I *don't* just think of you as someone who does porn," I said. "Or think of you differently. I mean, I guess technically now I think, 'Oh, Jonah does porn,' and that's different, but it's not like it matters."

He finally looked at me, eyebrows raised, and I grimaced.

"I mean, it *matters* because it's your job and stuff. I just mean that me telling you I didn't know about it wasn't because I think it's a big deal. I just... I don't deserve credit for being cool when I was just really, really stupid."

His laugh seemed to surprise him. "You're not stupid."

I snorted. "Well, I *did* think the whole 'pretend I have a boyfriend so my ex thinks I'm doing better than I actually am' thing would work. Which it did, I guess, but I still never figured out what you do from all the people who came in talking about you. Just that your name was Jonah."

"Really?" He took the drink and set it in front of him as he looked up at me. "One of your customers recognized me?"

"My customers? I think you mean your customers. Dante might as well rename this place the Fit and Flair Waiting Room. That's the only reason anyone comes here."

"I doubt that," he said.

"Well, it's not for the stellar drinks."

"I'm sure your drinks are fine."

As if to prove a point, he held my gaze as he leaned forward and put the straw in his mouth. Patiently, I watched as he took a long sip and swallowed.

To his credit, he fought wrinkling his nose as long as he could. But eventually he couldn't hold it back and I burst out laughing.

"I *told* you I suck at making drinks."

He tried to stifle a cough, his eyes sparkling as it turned into a laugh. "You don't suck. You just need a little... fine-tuning." He eyed the glass, then glanced at the bottles behind the bar. "Like, I'm pretty sure you're supposed to use peach schnapps, not peppermint."

"There are different kinds of schnapps?"

He opened his mouth, his shoulders lifting as he drew in a breath as if he was about to say something, but no words came out. After a moment, he pressed his lips together and I had no idea if he was trying not to laugh or not to cry.

"How mad will your boss be if I come back there and teach you how to make such a killer drink, you'll want to call it Making Sweet, Sweet Love On The Beach instead?"

A completely unrealistic vision of Jonah with his arms wrapped around me like he was trying to teach me how to swing a golf club, guiding my hands as I shook a martini shaker, fluttered through my mind.

"Probably not at all," I said. "Maybe he'll even print us new menus with that name."

ELEVEN

By the time Jonah was done with me, my Sex on the Beach was passable and I could make a pretty righteous layered Screaming Orgasm, though I still couldn't quite bring myself to say the name of it.

Then, once I'd promised to never, ever use a highball glass to scoop ice again after he spent almost fifteen minutes telling me a horror story of having a glass shatter in the ice bin, he taught me how to do a pour cut.

"If this is the Fit and Flair Waiting Room, you can give them a little preview," he'd said, and after a few tries using a bottle we'd refilled with tap water, I'd gotten pretty good at it.

That was more than I could say for the other trick he tried to teach me, which involved trying to flip the jigger from one hand to the other. I tried to tell him I wasn't coordinated enough for something like that, but he flashed that heart-melting smile at me and insisted it was easier than it looked.

On the first two attempts, the jigger bounced off my fingers and clattered onto the bar as I tried catching it.

"You're not putting enough force behind it," he said patiently, picking it up and handing it back to me. "Give it a bit more power so you're not having to move your hand to catch it."

"More power," I repeated. "Okay."

"You got this," he said.

"I got this."

And I did. I mean, if by "this," he'd meant "throw it way too hard so it smashed into the empty bottle we'd used for practicing pour cuts, making him lunge forward to catch said bottle before it toppled off the edge of the bar while the jigger fell to the ground and skittered under the ice bin."

Eyes wide, I stared at Jonah as he straightened up, then placed the empty bottle back on the bar.

"Maybe we shelve that one for now," he said lightly.

Then he glanced at me, I pressed my lips together, and we both burst out laughing.

"Why do you keep helping me?" I asked once we'd calmed down a bit and were leaning against the bar, the occasional giggle still hiccupping out of my throat.

"What do you mean?"

I picked up a cocktail napkin and dabbed the slight wetness beneath my eyes that had appeared after laughing so hard, my fingers cool against the warm pink of my cheeks. "Like teaching me this. Or how to make a drink that doesn't make you gag. And covering for me with the whole ex-boyfriend thing or getting that guy to leave me alone last night."

"There's a pretty big difference between showing you some bartending tricks and making sure some guy doesn't hurt you," he said. "Especially knowing Kyler's reputation."

"You know him?"

"He's a performer," he said. "The kind that gives the rest of us a bad name."

"Oh," I said. "Well, you still didn't have to do any of this."

He looked at me, rich chocolate eyes studying me with an almost-sad expression on his face. "I mean, sure. I didn't *have* to. But I would've been kind of an asshole to not help you when Kyler wouldn't let you go. And frankly, teaching you not to put peppermint schnapps in a Sex On The Beach was a public service. No one should have to suffer through that."

I started laughing again and he grinned.

"As for covering for you..." He shrugged, adjusting his stance so he could cross one ankle behind the other and bounce his toe on the ground. "I might not have *known* you, but you always seemed nice. You smiled at me a couple times and all that. And most nights, I see you busting your ass over here, looking flustered in this totally adorable way. When Grant said they'd just chatted with my girlfriend and pointed you out, you looked flustered in a different way and I just..."

He trailed off, which was probably a good thing because my head was already spinning as I processed his words.

"You... watch me?" I asked.

"Well, the walls are literally windows."

"Right. Of course." That didn't upset me at all, obviously. There was no reason for me to be upset by him clarifying he wasn't *looking* at me, just that I happened to be there.

But I guess it might have sounded like I was a little upset, because the corners of Jonah's mouth twitched into a small smile. "I mean, I'm not complaining about the view."

That made me roll my eyes. "You don't need to flatter me. I mean, you guys are always busy over there and it looks like you're having so much fun. And there's a veritable parade of hot girls coming here *just* to see you. I get it."

"Do you?" he asked.

"Of course."

"I don't think you do."

"Are you saying I'm a liar?"

He raised an eyebrow at me. "I'm saying the bartender across the way from where I work has the girl next door sort of vibe, you know? Killer curves, red hair, French braids, sort of breathlessly flustered but also a badass handling herself against all the drunk tourists? Not to mention that fucking adorable smile of yours. You're certifiably hot, Ginger Girl."

I didn't know what to say.

My heart was racing, hard enough that I was sure he would be able to see my pulse beating at the base of my neck. Jonah just called me hot. *Jonah.* Jonah Arizona, apparently known by many except me to be exceptionally good in bed. Jonah, who was literally hot for a living.

Jonah called me hot.

The statement broke my brain, which I think was fair given how... *unexpected* it had been. Before I could reboot my consciousness and come up with a response, though, Jonah stepped back and held up his hands in that reassuring way, his face sincere.

"Hey, I'm sorry. I'm not trying to, you know, make you uncomfortable or—"

"It's okay," I blurted. "I'm not, I just... I didn't expect—"

"I'm sorry," he repeated. "I sometimes forget people don't talk to each other the same way I might with like... you know. People I work with."

"It really is okay," I said, then grasped at the life preserver he didn't know he'd thrown to me. "But I do have a question about that, actually."

"About what?"

"Like, if you do..." I waved my hand at him, which was the gesture I'd apparently decided meant "porn." "... what you do, why do you work in a bar, too?"

"I'm also a personal trainer."

"You work *three* jobs?!"

He laughed. "Yeah. I'm so good at side hustles that I don't even have a main hustle, but I guess porn is probably the closest."

"Oh. Why don't you just pick one?"

"I get bored." He leaned back against the bar again. "Personal training can be hard with the hours to begin with, but when I started getting recognized a bit more often from being in porn, a lot of clients got weirded out. So I have a few regulars and I step in to help out some friends I have who still do it, but I like to keep it pretty casual. Then with porn itself, I'm kinda trying to get out of doing scenes and stuff with the studios, so—"

"You are?" I asked, surprised. "Like, you don't want to do it any-more?"

"Oh, I do," he said. "I dunno if I want to be a *performer* forever, but at this point I'm pretty committed to sticking in the adult industry somehow. But I like being my own boss. I make decent money doing my own thing and making my own videos. And I don't like a lot of the practices the studios have. It can be super toxic, which is why I want to stick around, you know? Help make things better."

He shrugged again.

"But it's not as lucrative as working with people like Grant, so when my roommate said they were looking for help here and it'd be perfect for me because I already knew how to juggle on account of the whole wanting to be a clown thing, I figured it wasn't a bad idea to pick up some shifts."

"Right," I said. "That all makes perfect sense."

"Does it?"

"Of course. All the cool kids go through a phase where they want to be a clown."

He burst out laughing. "I've never been a cool kid in my life. Just a giant dork."

I couldn't help smiling. "Why did you want to be a clown? Like, a circus clown, or...?"

"Yeah."

I clapped a hand to my mouth to hold back a giggle, but when Jonah shot me a playfully exasperated look, it escaped anyway.

"Give me a break," he said. "When I was a kid, I had it in my head that clowns were just like, the epitome of cool because they got to travel with the circus and party all the time. 'Cause they were always at birthday parties and stuff."

"And you thought that was the definition of partying?"

"I was eight years old," he repeated, wagging a finger at me. "And a fine, upstanding, well-behaved young man."

"Just like you are now?"

"I'm even better behaved now."

"That's too bad."

"Is it?" He flicked his eyebrows up and I felt myself turning red again.

"S-So you learned to juggle because you wanted to be a clown?"

He smiled. "Yeah. But then I ended up being pretty decent at it and kept at it. It was one of those things that you think will impress girls, but it really, really doesn't."

"I mean, I'm a little impressed."

Thank God I was wearing shorts and not a skirt because the look in Jonah's eyes could have made my panties drop all on their own. "Well, then it was all worth it."

TWELVE

I THINK THAT WAS around the time that Jonah realized I wasn't uncomfortable about flirting with him and that I was just horrendously, horrifically, to-my-core awkward.

How he realized that, I didn't know. Maybe it was the way I couldn't bring myself to look at him. Or the way I was blushing. Or maybe one of his many side hustles was mindreading and he could tell that I seriously considered looking up some of his work after I went home, and then immediately chided myself for seriously considering looking up some of his work.

Whatever it was, Jonah took pity on me and didn't draw attention to my awkwardness.

"The clown skills have also been surprisingly helpful for my solo content," he continued.

"What?"

"Yeah. A lot of people find naked juggling to be particularly captivating. And the ball jokes practically write themselves."

I giggled. "I guess there really is porn for everything."

"And then some."

Another quiet lull fell between us. I had more questions, but I couldn't quite bring myself to look at him while I asked them. Instead, I turned, trying to look casual as I picked up a bar rag and started cleaning the counter.

"So, how did you end up... doing that?" I asked.

"You can say the word, you know," he replied. "I heard you say it out loud not ten seconds ago."

I tried to keep myself from blushing. "How did you, um, end up doing porn?"

"You know how you get to that point where all your friends seem to know what they're doing with their lives and you're starting to freak out because you haven't figured it out yet?"

"Uh... sort of. I guess."

Jonah smiled. "That happened for me when I graduated college."

I paused, looking up at him. "You have a degree?"

"Don't sound so shocked," he said. "I'm more than a pretty face, you know."

"Oh, I didn't mean—"

"I'm joking, Ginger Girl," he said.

"Oh." I laughed softly and kept cleaning up the bar. "What's your degree in? Something to be a personal trainer?"

"Yeah," he said. "Exercise science, basically."

"So you're a naked juggler *and* a science nerd?"

He chuckled. "Yeah, totally. I dunno. Science is cool and I was into wrestling and football and stuff in high school, so when people started asking me what I was gonna do when I graduated, it made sense." He turned as he spoke, grabbing the containers of lemon and lime wedges and packing them up. "After I finished my degree, I was like... well shit. I don't know what to do next."

"I thought you wanted to be a personal trainer."

"That was more what I ended up doing," he said. "I didn't have any plans on what to *do* with the degree once I had it. So I ended up getting hired with this private gym as an onsite trainer, which was kind of a different set up, but it worked out okay. It wasn't paying all the bills and the owner was kind of a dick, but I had lots of people requesting me and stuff, so that was kind of cool."

"Sounds like you were pretty popular."

It was a bit surprising how humble he was about things. Jonah shrugged as he put the garnishes away in the fridge.

"I did alright. A lot of my clients were women, which I wasn't complaining about. Even if I wasn't going to do anything about it, because like I said—" He shot a shameless smile at me "—I was a fine, upstanding, well-behaved young man who didn't think it was right to get involved with clients."

"Were you actually?"

"For a while."

I laughed as I opened the small storage closet tucked behind the bar, tossing the dirty rag into the basket on the floor and grabbing the dilapidated broom. "But then...?"

"I had this one client. Chelsea." He stepped around me as I swept, opening the closet door without asking and grabbing fresh cleaning supplies. "She started requesting me every single time she came in and I wasn't going to pretend like I minded. She was a little crazy, a lot hot, and always wore a sports bra and short spandex shorts, regardless of if she was doing cardio or yoga or weight training."

"Ah," I said as I started sweeping.

Jonah shrugged and began sanitizing the soda nozzles. "I was twenty-two and spent most of my time in the gym. Everyone there was working up a sweat and getting in each other's spaces. As soon as Chelsea set her sights on me, I was doomed."

"You don't sound upset about it."

"Like I said. I was an idiot twenty-two-year-old. Constantly horny with a half-naked woman asking me to correct her posture when she was doing squats. I tried to pretend like I wasn't going to mix work and pleasure, but I'm also not going to apologize for giving in. If it bothers you, that kinda sucks, but I know I'm a decent guy and that everything was... you know, consensual and stuff."

I shook my head. "It's not bothering me. I just... how old are you now?"

"Twenty-seven," he said. "You?"

"Twenty-two."

"Oh." He started laughing. "I was immature at twenty-two. Doesn't mean everyone is. But I was. And I was restless, didn't know what I wanted to do, bored... you know? Like I said, I was starting to freak out because my friends seemed to be figuring their lives out and had girlfriends and were starting careers and I just had no idea what to do."

"So how did you get from personal training to porn?"

"I was training Chelsea one day, kinda near closing time. We were chatting and flirting while she was on the treadmill and I mentioned I used to wrestle in high school. She thought I meant entertainment wrestling and I told her no, I meant real wrestling. Then she said she'd never tried wrestling but she bet she could take me on, one thing led to another and we ended up in this private training room with wrestling mats on the floor."

I couldn't bring myself to look across the bar as I kept sweeping. "I think I see where this is going."

"If you don't want more details, I can stop," he said.

"No." The word surprised even me and I cleared my throat, which was suddenly dry. "I mean, you can keep going. Please."

Jonah was quiet for a moment, but not in an awkward way. Something tense and wonderful was filling the bar as we cleaned, something that felt anticipatory and intriguing, and when he spoke again, his voice had a smooth, inviting edge to it.

"Well, that was where it was going," he said. "We 'wrestled' for a while and I pinned her a couple of times, but I couldn't bring myself to... to *do* anything, even though I was pretty sure she wanted me to. So I had this brilliant idea to let her win and see what she did, which was a horrible idea on my part."

"Why?"

"Because she ended up on top of me, straddling my hips and... I mean, it was *very* clear that I wanted her to do something to me. I'm still not entirely sure that I let her win. She might've won fair and square, especially when she started... *moving*."

"Oh," I said.

"So this pretty little blonde woman is on top of me, pinning my arms down and grinding on me, leaning in so close that she could've kissed me, and I was more than happy to just lie there and let her. But she didn't like it that I'd let her win. She knew she had no chance at all since I was so much bigger than her, so she suggested that instead of going easy on her, maybe we needed to make things harder for me and I'd have to double pin her."

I dragged the broom across the same spot I'd swept three times already. "What's a double pin?"

"I didn't just have to pin her, I had to, uh... get *in* her."

My breath caught in my throat, settling on top of the warm heat that seemed to be rising in my chest. "Right. And... then what?"

"About thirty seconds later she ended up 'double pinned' face down on the mat with her shorts pulled halfway down her thighs and one of my arms around her chest."

I burst out laughing. "And then, let me guess, you ended up double-pinning her again, and again, and—"

Jonah had to rest a hand on the bar, he was laughing so hard. "Oh yeah. And then when I'd had about enough 'double-pinning' her into the mat, I let her up and she got on top of me and went to town, which is when the gym owner walked in."

I dropped the broom. "Oh, *no.*"

"That's what I thought," he said. "Though a little less politely. But as it turned out, he was a lot less of a dick to me when he realized I was perfect for his *other* business."

"What was his other business?"

Jonah raised his eyebrows at me.

"Oh," I said. "Right."

He chuckled. "He produced a kind of niche porn in the gym when they closed for the night, which was basically naked wrestling. When he asked if I wanted to give it a go, it was like something clicked. He sent me to get an STI panel done the next day and I had the results the day after that, which was good because I'd been a fucking moron with Chelsea and hadn't... you know. I wasn't thinking. But I got the all clear, so I showed up to the shoot that night with no idea what to expect. Like, I didn't even have a name. The guy who acted like the 'announcer' is going 'come on, man, we're trying to shoot, what's your name?' and I just said 'uh... Jonah?' and he switches to that like, loud announcer voice and goes 'Welcome to the ring, Jo-nahhh *Arizonaaaa*' and the rest, as they say..."

I snorted back a laugh. "I guess I should've known your real name isn't Jonah Arizona."

"Yeah, no. My parents didn't hate me *that* much."

I finished sweeping and looked up at him, suddenly as curious as I was concerned. "Do your parents know what you do?"

"Yeah," he said.

His tone was light enough that I grimaced. "Sorry. Do they not... I mean, you don't have to tell me. I don't mean to pry."

"No, it's okay," he said. "You're not prying. I never hid it from them. They were pretty shocked at first. My mom had a hard time with it because she was terrified she'd raised the kind of guy who would take advantage of women or whatever, even though I promised her I would *never* act like that. And Dad was upset because Mom was upset. But they've gotten oddly cool with it over the years. Mom warmed up a bit after I stopped doing the wrestling stuff."

"Why did you stop?"

He shrugged. "I saw it as more playful, fun, messing around sort of stuff. Like, I wasn't ever *actually* fighting with the girls. And I think they had fun with me because of it. But the guy who owned it, he wanted it to be more... forceful. And I'm not about that. So I didn't do stuff with that studio for very long and when I left, I was vocal about why. Between that and seeing how many people in the industry had no family or support system, I think they just accepted that it wasn't worth the risk of splitting our family up. So I've been pretty lucky."

He rolled his eyes.

"Now I just have to put up with my stupid brother making fun of me by calling me Jebraska Nebraska or Jontana Montana every time there's a family event."

THIRTEEN

LISTENING TO JONAH TALK was fascinating.

He lived a life that was incredibly different from anyone I'd ever met, and considering I lived in Vegas and met the most random of people every day, that was saying something. He wasn't ashamed of what he did for a living or the choices he made. If he made dumb choices, like not using a condom when he had sex with Chelsea, he called himself out on them and acknowledged how lucky he'd been.

For weeks, I'd viewed Jonah as someone so out of reach that he was almost mythical, more fantasy than factuality. But that was the Jonah I'd invented in my daydreams. The real Jonah was just as intriguing, but had the talent of making his life seem completely relatable even though I doubted anyone in the world could relate to half of what he said. He was funny and kind and helpful to the point of pitching in to clean the bar as I got ready to close. He did it in a way that seemed so natural, it wasn't until I went to fill the fridge with beer and mixers that I realized it was already restocked.

"Thank you," I said. "You didn't have to do all this."

He shrugged. "I was here and enjoying myself. It's no big deal. And this way when whoever's getting here to help you close shows up, you'll get home a little faster."

I stared at him. "What do you mean?"

"What do I mean what?"

"Why would anyone come help me close?"

It was his turn to stare at me, though there was a crease between his eyebrows as he did. "Uh... it's almost three a.m. in Vegas and you work at a busy bar on the Strip."

"I mean, it's not that busy. Normally I'm done just after three. I usually start cleaning a little earlier than I did tonight."

He opened his mouth, then closed it and glanced around. "You close by yourself? Every single night?"

"What's so hard to believe?" I asked, almost offended. "I work alone every single night."

"Yeah, I know, but I thought someone would come and... Jesus." He looked out the window at the mostly abandoned shops. "Do you have a... I dunno, a panic button or something?"

"Well... no."

"You should really talk to your boss."

"Oh, that's okay," I said. "It's not that bad."

He shook his head. "It is, though. You could get hurt."

"I'll be fine. I'm not scared or anything, Jonah. Nothing's ever gone wrong."

"Yeah, but something *could*. It's not worth risking it. Like, maybe you should consider calling the labour commissioner. I could back you up and—"

"No."

"Violet—"

"*No*," I repeated. "I can't call the labour commissioner."

"I feel like they might be concerned if you're working in dangerous conditions."

"I... I think they might be more concerned about, um, my ability to be working at all," I said as delicately as I could.

"Why would they—oh."

He stopped and stared at me. My throat felt tight and I glanced away, nerves making my spine tighten and shoulders tense.

"I won't say anything," he said.

I nodded, my neck stiff. "Thank you."

"You're not, like... stuck here or anything, are you?"

"No, I... No." I shook my head and sighed. "Yes and no. I should probably apply for a visa or something. I've just been scared that if I even ask, they'll send me away. And I have nowhere to go if they do, so I just... haven't."

"Alright," he said.

Then one of those awkward silences fell, heavy and uncomfortably consequential. After a moment, I cleared my throat and looked at the clock on the wall.

"Anyway, it's time for me to finish up," I said, walking towards the door with the assumption Jonah would follow. "I just need to get the register counted and then I'm leaving."

"How do you get home?" he asked.

"I drive."

"And you walk to your car? Alone?"

"It's fine. I'm over in the parking garage. It's a short walk and nothing bad has ever happened."

"Good," he said. "And nothing is ever going to. That's where we park too, so on nights I'm not here, one of the guys will stick around and walk with you."

I whirled around. Jonah was still standing by the bar, arms crossed across his chest as he leaned back against it casually.

"Fit and Flair closes at two," I said. "They can't stay late for me. *You* can't stay late for me."

"We close at two but someone's usually here until two-thirty or quarter to three closing up. It won't kill anyone to wait fifteen minutes to walk a hot redhead to her car."

Oh, God. He'd already figured out I swooned helplessly whenever he called me hot. Willing myself not to blush, I folded my arms and gave him the sternest look I could manage.

"I can take care of myself, you know."

"I do know," he said patiently. "I've watched you do it. Frankly, you could probably protect us better than we could protect you. But we don't work alone, and none of us walk alone to our cars either."

"Exactly. *You* don't work alone. I do. We aren't co-workers, Jonah."

"Didn't you say this is the Fit and Flair Waiting Room?"

The question threw me off. "I... yes, I guess I did."

He flashed me a smile. "So that means we might as well be co-workers. We're close enough, at least."

I tried to come up with a response, but Jonah's smile flustered me as much as his words did. When I couldn't think of an argument, I sighed.

"Has anyone ever told you that you're bossy?" I asked as I locked the door with him still standing by the bar.

"In my industry, they usually say 'dominant,'" he replied, and my heart raced so fast that I had to recount the till three times before I realized I was mistaking the dimes for nickels.

FOURTEEN

"WELL, WOULD YOU LOOK at that," I said as we approached my car. "Nothing bad happened."

There were still plenty of cars parked in the employee lot, but Jonah and I were the only people on that level of the parking garage, which wasn't unusual. I was sure there were plenty of other people who finished work around the same time as me, but I rarely ran into anyone on my way back to my car. When I did, half the time it was one of the security guards.

"We still have a ways to go," Jonah said, even though it was very clear that the car parked three stalls away from where we were was mine, given that I'd pressed the key fob and it had blinked the parking lights twice. "Don't jinx it."

I tried not to laugh as we reached the parking spot next to mine. "How about now?"

"Hmm. Still sketchy." He reached my car and pressed his face up to the rear passenger window, covering the sides of his eyes with his hands.

The attempt not to laugh failed. "What are you doing?"

He made a show of checking that side, then the passenger window, and then crossing around to the driver's side, peering in with his face pressed to the glass even though I didn't have tinted windows and the fluorescent lights of the parking garage clearly illuminated the crumpled McDonald's bags and empty Gatorade bottles discarded in the backseat of my car.

"Checking for trespassers," he said, then straightened up and slapped a hand to the roof of the car. "She's all clear, boss. Permission to board."

"I need permission to get into my own car now?" I asked, amused. "Or was that you asking for permission to get in so I can bring you to your car?"

As skilled at flustering me as Jonah seemed to be and as many things as I'd said that apparently surprised him, I hadn't been able to fluster him back until then. Glancing to the side, he laughed awkwardly.

"Uh, no, it's okay," he said. "I didn't drive."

I frowned. "How are you getting home, then?"

"I told my roommate to take off without me," he said. "But it's cool. I was just gonna grab an Uber."

I raised my eyebrows, then shook my head as I moved to meet him on the driver's side. "Get in."

"What?"

"I'll drive you home."

"It's okay, you don't have to—"

"Didn't you *just* say you guys don't walk alone, either?" I asked.

He grimaced. "I mean, yeah, but—"

"And you're only stuck here because you stayed late after I dragged you into my ex-boyfriend drama."

"I chose to stay late to hang out with you," he said.

"That doesn't change the fact you don't have a ride home."

"Violet," he said, and I tried not to shiver at the sound of my name rolling around his mouth. "I don't want you to go out of your way on my behalf."

"Jonah," I replied with what I thought was a steady, patient tone. "You helped me so much tonight. Consider it payback, okay? For teaching me how to have a screaming orgasm—*make*." The word came out loud, echoing through the parking garage as I tried to cover my mistake. "Make a... a Screaming... you know."

His mouth twitched as he tried not to laugh. "It's just payback for that?"

I cringed. "I don't know why I picked that one specifically. Please just tell me where you live before I die of embarrassment."

He laughed, but at least he finally listened to me. His address wasn't too far out of the way—I mean, it was a good fifteen minutes from where I lived, but it wasn't like he lived on the complete other side of Clark County or something—and I only had to ask two more times before he walked around to get into the passenger seat while I slouched into the driver's.

"You wanna put my address in your phone?" he asked as he climbed in.

"Yeah, in a sec," I said, pulling my phone out of my purse so I could plug it into the charger. "Let me just make sure Rico absolutely doesn't need a ride before I leave."

"Rico?"

"My roommate."

"Ah," he said. "The drag queen? Faye?"

"That's the one," I said distractedly as I typed a quick message. *Still assuming you don't need a ride. I'm giving Jonah a ride home. Have fun with Clark/Vanessa.* "I pick him up on nights he's performing usually, but he's probably going to his..."

I stopped, thinking for a moment.

"I don't know if he's Rico's boyfriend yet, but it's the second night in a row he's spending there, which might be a record for Rico. Though, I guess it might just be because the afterparty thing keeps running late." I handed my phone to Jonah so he could plug his address in. "Speaking of which, why aren't you there?"

"They gave me Friday off from the bar but couldn't swing Saturday," he replied as he typed. "But I got what I needed from it. I made it to at least part of each day and networked with who I needed to last night."

I wondered vaguely if "networked" was code for something, but decided my blood pressure couldn't handle me asking outright.

"What kinds of people do you network with?" I asked instead as he put my phone in the mount on the dashboard so I could see the GPS.

"All sorts. Industry contacts, producers, studio reps, other performers. Anyone who it's good to keep in touch with for whatever reason."

I nodded slowly as I pulled out of my parking spot. "Is it weird? Seeing all those people you've... you know."

"Fucked?"

I wrinkled my nose and he laughed.

"Not really," he said. "It's just sex, you know? The only time it's weird is when you run into someone you might've had something more than a working relationship with, but I feel like that's true of any industry."

"Like you ran into your ex-girlfriend?"

"Sort of. Not really. It's complicated," he said as I turned down the ramp to leave the garage. "Ex-friends-with-benefits would probably be most accurate. It's just hard to make things work in this industry. You end up with people who do the same things you do because no one else is interested in anything serious with people who sell sex for a living. But even though people say there won't be any jealousy or issues, there always are when things get more serious and since everything ends up being connected, it gets complicated." He laughed quietly. "I've dated here and there, but not anything serious in a few years."

"Do you miss it?"

"Being in a relationship?"

"Yeah."

"A little."

"Oh. I'm sorry."

"Nothing to be sorry for." He leaned back in the passenger seat. "It's an expected consequence of what I do. Anyway, enough about me, Ginger Girl. I've been blabbing about myself all night."

I smiled, pulling up to a light and flicking my turn signal on. "I like hearing about you. You're interesting."

"And so are you." He smiled at me. "Besides, I should probably know a bit more about my fake girlfriend and all. So, let's start with that asshole from earlier. Trevor? How'd you meet him?"

Of course he wanted to know about Trevor.

FIFTEEN

THE SMILE FADED OFF my face, but if Jonah noticed, he didn't say anything. I hesitated, almost telling him I didn't *want* to talk about it... but that wasn't the truth.

Sure, I might have just met him, but he made me feel like he'd understand. Like he wouldn't be judgemental.

Like I was safe to share that part of my life with him.

"Trevor and I..." I started, then sighed. "We were high school sweethearts."

"High school—wait." He turned in place, his surprise so evident I could see it from the corner of my eye. "*How*—"

"We moved here together," I said. "From a small town in Saskatchewan."

"Where's—"

"Canada."

"Right. That probably made me sound pretty stupid."

I shrugged. "Most people here have no idea where it is."

"So you... both came here? Without visas?"

"He had one. I didn't. It was not my smartest moment." I sighed again. "But I really thought I loved him. When he told me he was leaving for

Vegas, I wasn't thinking about things like visas or how to apply for them or anything. I just begged him to take me along. If he hadn't..."

I paused, biting my lip as I remembered the day Trevor had shown up at my parents' place to tell me he was leaving. Sitting on my bed with its threadbare blankets and lumpy pillows, crying, sobbing, pleading with him even as he protested, until he was crying just as hard and hugging me, kissing me, apologizing to me.

"Please don't leave me here," I had said. "Even if you don't love me anymore, just don't... don't leave me here."

"You think I don't love you anymore?" Trevor had asked.

Sniffling, I wiped my tears on my sleeve. "Why else wouldn't you want me to come?"

"Vi, I love you. I *love* you. I just... I don't know if I can take care of both of us." He covered my hand with his, looking down at them with his cheeks flushed red. "I don't want to put you into an even worse situation than you're in now. At least here, you have a home and friends and—"

"No, I don't. And now I won't have you."

"I'm sorry." He wrapped his arms around me, his face buried in my hair. We sat like that, just breathing, just holding each other in heart-breaking silence.

"If this is really it," I finally said. "Can... can we sleep together?"

Trevor's arm dropped from my shoulders. "Can we... what?"

My cheeks burned. "I still want my first time to be with you. Even if you... if you don't want to get married anymore or... or if you're not coming back for me."

"Violet, I—"

But I was already shaking my head, pushing myself away and standing up. "No, you're right. That was... I shouldn't have—"

Before I could finish dying of embarrassment, though, my bedroom door banged open and my nightmare flew in, certain that she'd caught me and Trevor in the act of doing what I'd just proposed. As usual, she screamed, and as usual, Trevor left so that she'd calm down, and as usual, it didn't work even though I'd told him every time it happened that she stopped calling me those horrible things as soon as he'd went away.

I just didn't want him to be around to hear it.

But this time, Trevor hadn't actually left. This time, after she went back to the living room to drink herself into a slumber and I'd huddled on my bed, trying to stop the tears from coming, Trevor came around to my bedroom window and tapped until I opened it up.

"We... we can get married one day," he said. "Just grab your stuff and come with me."

I didn't give Jonah all those details, though. Just the ones I could stand to speak out loud.

"We looked out for each other," I said. "We were the outsiders. Trevor was the gay kid. He said he was bisexual, but I think that was probably just to make his life the tiniest bit easier because then he could use me as a cover and wear my clothes."

"Wear your... what?"

"Drag," I said. "Saskatchewan's pretty conservative and his parents were not exactly supportive of him. I wanted to be the one who believed in him and helped him achieve his dreams, so when he'd come over, I'd help him do makeup and hide his drag outfits and stuff." I smiled in spite of myself. "It was fun, honestly."

"Why were you an outsider?" he asked.

"We were... poor." I thought of my nightmare again, the woman who was supposed to be on my side and who never once had been. "My mom had a drinking problem. My dad left her and wouldn't pay child support because he thought things like college were a waste of money for women since we just get married and pop out babies so our husbands are stuck paying all the bills for the rest of our lives."

Jonah winced. "Yikes."

"Yeah. So I was the smelly kid who wore old clothes and never got to go on class field trips because they cost too much."

"Damn. That sucks."

"Yep. So when Trevor said that Vegas would be where he got his big break in drag, I begged to come with him because I didn't want to get left behind in that stupid town. It was... I didn't leave on good terms." I shook my head. "I didn't leave on any terms, actually, but my mom called when she realized she hadn't seen me around for a few days and said... well, it boiled down to telling me not to bother coming back. So after Trevor and I broke up, I had nowhere to even go back to. If it wasn't for Rico, I don't know what I would've done."

"How did you meet Rico?"

"Trevor cheated on me with him."

"He did *what*?!"

I burst out laughing. "Rico didn't know about me. He put it together after Trevor and I ran into him on the Strip one night. After that, he took me home with him and helped me get a job. He said he'd make sure Trevor never did drag in Vegas again but I asked him not to."

Jonah snorted. "You're far too nice."

"Maybe." I twisted my mouth to the side. "I might be bitter about everything, but I understand, at least a little. I was naïve. Trevor was scared. Growing up where we did, I know why he felt like he couldn't tell the truth. I just wish he would've at least told me before I came here with him. I would've still come, but it wouldn't have hurt so much, you know? We would've just had each other's backs. I don't know why he felt like he had to lie."

"He's an idiot," Jonah said decisively.

"He can't help who he is. And he helped me, too."

"Those things aren't mutually exclusive. Like, whatever his sexuality is, he missed out on having an amazing person in his life. And sure, he might have helped you. But he hurt *you*." Jonah folded his arms across his chest. "Ergo, idiot. You can trust me. I'm a scientist."

I giggled. "I don't know about 'amazing.' If you think I'm awkward and weird now, you should've seen me before Rico got his hands on me."

"I don't think you're awkward or weird, Ginger Girl."

The words came out soft but sincere. Outside the car, streetlights cast golden streaks through the windshield, growing and fading as I drove, filling the car as much as our silence did.

And maybe it was just the moment. Maybe it was that telling someone about my stupid childhood and stupid parents and stupid ex-boyfriend had my heart feeling a little raw and I was putting far too much stock in what he said. Maybe it was just that he'd told me so much about himself and I'd told him about myself and even though we'd technically met for the first time that night, it felt like we knew each other a lot better. It could have even been that I was hoping for something that wasn't there, that I was assigning a meaning to his words he hadn't intended.

It was probably that last one that tore a hole right through my personal filter.

"I liked the kiss," I blurted.

SIXTEEN

"WHAT?" HE ASKED.

My face burned and words poured out of my mouth, even as my mind screamed for me to shut up.

"When you kissed me. I liked it. You're really good at kissing and I just wanted you to know that even though you didn't mean it, I liked it. No one's ever kissed me like that before and I know it probably means nothing coming from me when you do far more than kiss people for a living, but I just... I wanted you to know that you know what you're doing and it's... hot."

"I mean, if I knew what I was doing, I wouldn't be working three jobs and living in a house with two other porn stars," he said, gentle laughter in his voice. "But thank you. I'm... I'm glad you thought it was hot."

Is there anything worse than that?

I mean, yes, there are plenty of things that are worse, I guess. But at the time, I felt like that was about the worst thing I could have heard.

He was glad *I* thought it was hot. Because he didn't. Because he was trying to be nice and not tell me that I kissed like a particularly skittish hamster or something.

And he was probably regretting calling me hot all those times because now he had the job of trying to let me down gently, even though he shouldn't have to because I *knew* he was out of my league and still had let myself get to know him and now it was awkwardly silent in the car again.

Ugh.

I grimaced, turning my signal on to switch into the right lane.

"Um..." he said.

"Huh?"

"I... I live that way."

I glanced at my GPS. I had to go left to get to Jonah's place, not right as if I was going to mine. Swallowing hard, I shoulder checked even though there were no other cars on the road before moving to the left lane. Face still red, I stopped at the lights, my fingers curled tightly around the steering wheel.

"Sorry. Habit," I forced myself to say.

"It's okay."

I tried to laugh. "I told you I wasn't cool."

"What?"

I tapped my fingers on the wheel. "Awkward, weird, uncool. Take your pick."

He was quiet for a moment. "Well, you're wrong. I do think you're pretty cool. I'm just very aware that I'm in a small, enclosed space with you and the last thing I want to do is come onto you if that's not something you want. I don't want you to be uncomfortable."

Holy shit.

I mean, holy *shit*.

"Uncomfortable how?" I asked.

"Like... I wouldn't want to make you uncomfortable by saying if you somehow forgot you were driving to my place, which is a shitty house with two roommates who will make things awkward if I show up with a girl that one of them definitely would recognize and has talked about how fucking gorgeous she is before, and instead went to your place, where your roommate is for sure not home yet... I'm just saying, I'd probably want to kiss you again to prove that I definitely meant it the first time, too."

Oh God.

"And that I also thought it was insanely hot."

Oh my *God*.

"And that getting to know you tonight has been the most fun I've had in ages, and considering I fuck for a living, that's saying something."

It took a moment before my thoughts were comprehensible as words again.

Jonah wanted to... well, to at least kiss me again, but if he was asking me to go to my place, he was probably thinking about doing a lot more than just kissing. I mean, if he just wanted to kiss, we could've done that in the car outside his place. But to go to my place? Where there were no annoying roommates? Where I would have the apartment to myself with a man who liked me, who actually *liked* me and laughed at my jokes and—

And he fucked for a living.

It wasn't that he had sex with other people, or in front of a camera, or anything like that. I wasn't worried that he'd give me something. I knew where Rico kept the condoms and from what Jonah had said earlier, he got tested regularly.

It was that he fucked for a living, and I was a goddamn virgin who had no idea what she was doing.

But it was like the girl from the birthday party had said earlier when she claimed Jonah was her hall pass. Sort of, anyway. I mean, if I was going to lose my virginity, why shouldn't it have been with someone who knows what they're doing? With someone who was *good* at it? And that all made sense, of course, but...

But what if Jonah didn't want to?

What if he thought it was weird, or too much pressure, or—

"Violet?" he said, breaking me out of my thoughts. "The light's green."

I stared up at the stoplight, which was indeed green, but I didn't take my foot off the brake. There was no one behind me. No one beside me. The road was, for all intents and purposes, deserted.

"I don't want you to feel pressured," he said.

"I'm not," I finally managed to say. "I... I want to turn right, but if I do it without telling you something, you're going to be mad. And if I tell you, you're probably going to make me turn left."

"And right is...?"

"To my place. To... you know."

"Show you how to have a Screaming Orgasm?"

I laughed. It came out more like a hysterical cackle, but it was a laugh all the same.

"Try me, Ginger Girl," he said. "Tell me what you have to tell me."

"I've never had sex before."

The words hung between us, a silent echo bouncing off the windshield as the stoplight changed to yellow, then to red. Jonah took a deep breath, then blew it out loudly.

"Sheesh," he said. "Yeah, that's... that's not a dealbreaker, Ginger Girl."

I winced. "I'm sorry. I *knew* you'd think it was an issue and even though I don't want to—wait."

He burst out laughing.

"It's *not* a dealbreaker?" I asked.

"Nah," he said, still chuckling. "Like, the way you're acting, I kind of suspected. And I'll probably ask you about thirty times if you're sure because you only have one virginity or whatever and like, *you're* the one who would have to live with losing it to someone who does porn. And I mean, if you're only wanting to do this because there's some kind of clout or something to being with a 'porn star,' then I'd probably say no, but—"

"It has nothing to do with you being a porn star," I interrupted. "I want to have sex with you because you're hot and nice and I... I've wanted to for two weeks without even *knowing* you did porn. I mean, yes, if I'm being honest, it's kind of comforting to know that you know what you're doing and are probably really good at it, but I'd still want to even if it turned out that you suck at sex."

"I believe you, Ginger Girl," he said. "You just said 'sex' and 'porn' six or seven times without stammering, so it's obvious you mean it."

"I do," I said, my voice wavering.

"So, I'm into it. On one condition."

"What's that?"

"Look at me."

I frowned, turning my head. "Is that the condition?"

"No." He looked directly into my eyes, his face serious. "I don't care if I'm literally, like, cock lined up ready to start fucking you or buried balls deep. Whether it's the moment we pull up to your place or right when we're about to come. If you change your mind, I need you to tell me. Please."

"I will," I promised.

"Immediately," he said. "Don't feel like you can't say no or stop me or something, okay? That's... I know there's a stigma around male performers doing shit without consent, and I don't ever, *ever* want to be that guy, even unintentionally."

"I promise, Jonah," I repeated.

He licked his lips, his eyes flicking down to mine and making my stomach flutter.

"Alright," he said. "So? Left or right?"

The light turned green again and I flipped my signal on, cutting across three empty lanes to turn right.

SEVENTEEN

I USED TO THINK I'd lose my virginity in a heart-shaped bed.

I don't know *why* I was so sure the bed would be heart-shaped. Somewhere along the line, I'd probably watched some cheesy romantic movie where the honeymoon suite had a heart-shaped bed and made the assumption that all honeymoon suites had heart-shaped beds.

Because until I broke up with Trevor, I thought it would be to him. I really, truly, honestly thought we were waiting until marriage. Where I grew up, that was the narrative: you didn't have sex until your wedding night. Sure, most people didn't stay virgins until they were married, but most people weren't the smelly girl who lived in a ramshackle double-wide that should've probably been condemned before she was even born.

Regardless, I thought losing my virginity would involve lacy lingerie and a bottle of champagne and chocolate covered strawberries. Garter belts and flowers and unclasping lines of tiny buttons along the back of a white dress. Plush blankets and fluffed pillows, quiet embraces, slow and passionate thrusts that were contradictory in their confidence since neither of us would actually *know* what we were doing, but that didn't matter in my daydreams.

Maybe, if Trevor hadn't let me believe we would get married one day, I would've had a different daydream. Instead of a traditional wedding night, I might have thought I'd lose my virginity curled up on a couch in someone's basement, cozy and safe and warm. On a beach, maybe, or even a hotel room that *didn't* have a heart-shaped bed.

But I probably wouldn't have daydreamed about losing my virginity in a bedroom that was more like a walk-in closet with a full size bed crammed in the corner.

That seemed to be what was happening, though. After parking my car and assuring Jonah, not for the last time, that I was sure about this, I led him up to my apartment and unlocked the door with shaking hands.

"Damn it, Rico," I said as the door swung open and a wall of cold air blasted me in the face.

"Whew," Jonah said, shivering.

I hung my keys on the hook by the door and rushed towards the thermostat so I could turn the air conditioning down. "He always turns the AC up while he's getting in drag so he doesn't sweat his makeup off while it's setting, but then conveniently manages to forget to turn it back to non-hypothermic levels when he's done."

"Makes sense," Jonah said as closed the door and, in an oddly familiar sort of way, locked it behind him before looking at me.

"Sorry," I said. "It shouldn't take long to warm up."

"I can think of a way to stay warm in the meantime," he replied.

My breath caught in my throat.

"Unless you've changed your mind, which—"

"Come warm me up."

He chuckled as he walked slowly towards me. "God, I was hoping you'd say that."

"I'm sure about this," I promised him.

He stopped in front of me, the corners of his rich brown eyes crinkling as he looked at me. "So you want me to kiss you again?"

"Yes."

"Good," he said, and then his lips were on mine.

God, could he kiss. His lips made me feel like I was slipping underwater, my hearing suddenly silenced and a wash of pressure surrounding me. The warmth of his mouth was both captivating and comforting, something that soothed me while it awakened me. That sensation of being caressed was heightened from the first time he'd kissed me, probably because this time he *was* caressing me, his fingers tracing the spot on my neck just below my hairline.

His body was closer this time, his chest against mine and his hips inching forward until they were touching me. He used his body to walk me back against the wall, then pinned me in place as he let every inch of himself rest against me.

Until then, I'd been quiet, the occasional intake of breath the only noise I made as he guided me towards the moment I wanted *so* much. But once I was pressed against the wall, he rested the hand that wasn't on my neck just to the side of my face. Even though we were the same height, the action made me feel small in the best way, like he was towering over me not to devour me but to shield me, to center me, to block out any thoughts I had except what he was about to do to me.

Then he slipped his tongue in my mouth and I broke my silence with a whimper.

Jonah responded with a noise of his own, a soft *mmm* sound that vibrated against my mouth. His tongue danced along my lower lip, tracing it before sliding between my lips again so it could meet mine. I shivered, the feel of his tongue and the subtle taste of his mouth alluring and exciting, and another quiet moan slipped out.

"You okay?" he murmured against my lips.

"Uh-huh," I managed to grunt, which made him smile.

"Wanna take this somewhere else?"

"Yeah."

He stopped pressing me to the wall and I led him down the short hallway to my bedroom. It wasn't until I opened the door and Jonah glanced in that I realized I should probably explain why most of my room was overstuffed with clothes racks and stacks of stilettos lining the walls.

"It's... Rico needs space for his... stuff," I said.

Jonah gazed into the room, his eyes widening. "I can see why."

"Sorry."

"For what?"

"It's not the most, um, romantic place," I said, then laughed awkwardly. "Not that it matters much. I mean, it's just... you know. That was stupid."

"It wasn't stupid."

"I just sleep in here," I said, not sure why I felt the need to explain. "And he's really good about it. Like, he doesn't get mad if I look through it or come in here without asking and he doesn't charge me much in rent because I'm okay with sharing the room. And I don't usually, you know, bring people... here. Ever, actually. So I didn't, um—"

"Vi, I share a room with a guy who tests and reviews pretty much every Bad Dragon product you can think of," Jonah said. "You don't have to justify it to me if it works for you, okay?"

I nodded, my cheeks warm. "Do I want to know what Bad Dragon is?"

"Depends. How weirded out are you by people fucking things with tentacles and scales?"

I opened my mouth, then closed it, and Jonah dissolved into laughter. His arm moved around my waist and he pulled me in close, kissing me again as we stood in the doorway to my room.

"Still doing okay?" he asked.

"Sort of," I replied.

He stopped kissing me and looked up, his eyes serious and attentive.

"I haven't changed my mind," I continued. "I just, um, want to... to use the bathroom. Give me a couple of minutes?"

"Of course," he said. "Take all the time you want."

Eighteen

I DIDN'T *WANT* TO take any time at all away from his lips and hands and body, but I did *need* to. Leaving Jonah in my room, I crossed the hall to the bathroom I shared with Rico and closed the door.

Holy shit, I was doing this.

I was excited.

Almost completely excited. I mean, mostly excited, and a little nervous.

A good amount nervous, actually.

A... a lot nervous.

Maybe afraid? I stared at myself in the mirror, then shook my head. No, not afraid. I trusted Jonah. Maybe it was strange to trust him so quickly after meeting him, but I did, plain and simple. So I was nervous and excited, and those two things made sense because I was about to...

I was going to have sex with him.

Thinking the words made my stomach tingle. I was going to kiss him, get naked with him, touch him and stroke him and have part of him *inside* of me. I bit my lip, but even as I did, a smile started spreading across my face.

Okay. I was mostly excited.

I washed up, then unbraided my hair and shook it out, letting it fall in crinkled waves around my shoulders. Rico and I each had a drawer to ourselves in the bathroom and we generally didn't snoop through each other's things, but he'd told me multiple times that he always kept a box of condoms in his drawer.

"Help yourself if you ever decide to get someone to turn you from a sponge cake to a Twinkie," he'd teased, and as many times as I'd rolled my eyes at him, I was thankful for the half-empty box tucked between his shaving kit and multiple half-filled bottles of cologne. I tucked a few condoms in my pocket, not sure if I was being overly cautious or overly ambitious, and took a final deep breath.

"I can do this," I whispered to myself, then went to join Jonah in my room.

He turned just as I re-entered and froze in place. He'd moved one of the flimsier clothes racks in front of the window, then found a bolt of gauzy pink fabric Rico had tucked into the corner and hung some of it over the rack so that the streetlight filtering in from the blinds gave the room a soft, glowy feel. On the clothing rack across from my bed, he'd discovered Rico's tulle ballgown that had LED lights built into the skirt and had wrestled it out so he could hang it sideways, flaring the skirt out to cover as much of the clothes rack as it could.

"Okay, it was the best I could do for romance on short notice, but..."

He reached over to the small stool I used as a nightstand and switched off the desk lamp I had sitting there, leaving the room swathed in soft pinpricks of light and a filtered golden glow.

"It's kinda like candlelight, maybe?" he said.

I looked around. The warm feeling in my stomach spread to my chest and, oddly enough, made a lump in my throat.

"It's like stars," I said softly.

Jonah smiled and crossed the small room so he was in front of me again.

"Every first time deserves a little romance," he said. "Even if you might have to be, uh... creative about it."

"So I can pretend you're gonna make love to me on a blanket under the stars?" I joked.

The light reflecting off Jonah's eyes gave him a wicked look, especially when he licked his lips like he did just then.

"Oh, no," he said. "I'm not gonna make love to you. I'm gonna blow your mind."

"Are you?" I asked breathlessly.

"Yep." His lips were almost on mine. "See, here's the thing, Ginger Girl. That douchebag you used to date? He only got you because your standards were buried six feet under. So I'm gonna show you how you're *supposed* to be treated and ruin you for any guy that might come next. I mean, I'm kinda hoping *I'm* the guy who comes next, but just in case I'm not, I need to set the bar high enough that you won't ever be able to settle for a man who doesn't deserve you again."

I hadn't noticed his hand creeping around my waist again until just then, when he used it to pull my body against his.

"So no, I'm not gonna 'make love' to you," he said. "I'm going to fucking *worship* you."

And oh, did he.

My head spun as he kissed me again, so hard and so passionately that I could barely draw in a breath. He let go of my waist so he could cradle my head in his hands, his thumbs on my cheeks and his lips devouring mine as he pressed our bodies together. A soft moan left my throat and he raked his teeth across my bottom lip, then traced the same path with his tongue before flicking it against mine.

Those ceaseless kisses didn't stop as his hands left my face and moved down to my shoulders, then slipped down my arms before finding the bottom of my black t-shirt.

"Can I take this off?" he whispered.

I shivered as his fingers played along the hem. "Yes."

He tugged it up, moving at a tantalizingly slow pace as the cool air surrounding us hit the heated skin on my stomach. Another breath hitched as he peeled it up further, and further, until my ribs were bared, then he was pulling it over my bra-clad breasts.

"One sec," he said against my lips, then began to move away.

I clutched at him. "No. Please don't stop kissing me."

He chuckled, then nipped my lip again.

"This is the hardest one," he said, tugging at my t-shirt. "Once this is off, I can kiss you forever, if you want."

As if to punctuate his sentence, he kissed me again, but I wasn't quite convinced.

"What about when you have to take your shirt off?"

"Good point." He began to lift my shirt. "Arms up. Take this off, then you can do mine, and then I'll kiss you until you can't think so logically anymore."

And suddenly, the prospect of needing to stop kissing him didn't matter so much, because Jonah was about to be shirtless.

Obediently, I lifted my arms, and Jonah laughed again before carefully stripping my t-shirt off. He let it fall to the floor and pressed a quick kiss to my lips before stepping back and letting his eyes flick down to take in the partially illuminated sight of me in my bra and jean shorts.

"Good news," he said. "I was right. You're *incredible*."

"I'm alright," I said, blushing.

"Are you kidding? Look at this." Jonah traced a hand along my side, from just above the waistband of my jeans to just beneath my bra. "This is the optimal curve."

"The *what*?!"

He grinned. "The curve that corresponds to the ideal optimum value. Which, in this case, is how fucking sexy your body is."

"I... uh..." I stammered as he trailed his fingers back down my stomach, shivers branching out from his feather-light touch. "Are you hitting on me with math?"

"Of course not. I'm complimenting you with math." He reached for me with his other hand, cupping the soft dip of my waist and squeezing. "Because that means it's not just my opinion, Ginger Girl. It's a verifiable fact that you are, as we scientists say, fucking delectable."

I didn't know what to say. My face was turning red, I was sure, and my stomach was filled with flutters. Jonah stepped forward, placing a gentle kiss on my lips.

"You're gorgeous, Violet."

"You are, too," I whispered, then swallowed nervously. "Can I, um, do yours now?"

He nodded and I reached for the hem of his t-shirt. He waited as I lifted over his stomach, my fingertips brushing against hard muscle, then obediently raised his arms so I could pull it over his head. Just as the shirt covered his eyes, I snuck a quick glance down to check him out while he couldn't see me.

Which I shouldn't have done.

"Oh my God!" I gasped, abandoning my task as my eyes widened.

NINETEEN

"WHAT'S WRONG?" JONAH ASKED, his alarmed voice muffled by the t-shirt that was now stuck over his head.

Without even thinking to ask, I touched his ribs. "Scrabble Guy!"

He burst out laughing and reached up to finish the job I'd abandoned the moment I saw the tattoos on his ribs and *finally* realized why everyone called him Scrabble Tiles.

The tattoo was lovely, done in black and grey with sharp, crisp lines. The tiles spilled out from a sketched bag, tumbling down his ribcage and into a jumbled pile on the side of his stomach. I didn't have any tattoos myself, but I'd always thought they were interesting and loved looking at them on other people. And this?

This was one of the coolest ones I'd ever seen.

"I got it before I started performing," he explained as I examined the tattoo.

"Does it mean something?

"Mostly that Scrabble is my favourite board game."

I traced the letter in the pile, my fingers staggering as I belatedly realized I was *touching* his chest. His skin was warm and smooth beneath my fingertips and I was distracted for a moment by the sight of his muscles: a hard, flat stomach and defined pecs with a few other tattoos on his chest.

If he had chest hair, he removed it, which probably had to do with the whole porn thing, but there were freckles scattered across his ribs and stomach that made his perfect body just a bit more relatable.

A bit more inviting.

Especially because I had the oddest urge to connect each of those freckles with my tongue.

"But it does have a hidden meaning," Jonah continued, gently putting his hand around my wrist and guiding my hand and my attention back to his tattoo. "The 'Scrabble Tiles' thing started because everyone thought I had the wrong numbers on them, but the letters are initials." He set my hand on one set of falling tiles, which read E and D. "That's my mom, and her birth year." He moved it to another set, reading G and D. "Dad and his year." Then to the third, which was J and D. "My brother, who unfortunately has the same initials as me, but no one except them knows what they mean anyway."

"I love it," I said, grinning as he let go of my hand so I could trace the tiles all over again. "And I'm glad I was wrong about the existence of a sexy Scrabble tournament."

He put his hands on my hips and pulled me in. "Never say never. Maybe that'll be my next side hustle. Naked juggling and sexy Scrabble."

I was still giggling when he kissed me again, though the giggles didn't last long. Not when suddenly there was hard muscle and smooth skin pressed against me, when I could feel the warmth of his skin with my own, and when his hands moved from my hips to the back of my jean shorts to carefully cup my ass.

"Still good?" he asked.

"Uh-huh," I breathed.

"Good," he said, then groaned as his hands tightened on my ass. "God, Violet. You're addictive."

He kept kissing me, though his lips left my mouth and peppered soft kisses along my chin and down my neck. I inhaled sharply as he found a spot that made electricity shoot through my body, then quivered when he tongued that same spot, and full-on moaned when he sucked on it.

"Jesus," I whimpered. "What are you—*oh*!"

I felt his smile as he sank his teeth into it lightly. My body seemed to *love* that and even as moved away so he could place open-mouthed kisses along my neck, I could feel heat tingling and radiating from that first spot.

"You like that?"

"Uh-huh," I said.

"Am I making you wet?" he asked.

"I mean, your mouth is kinda wet, but—"

"Violet," he said, his voice stern. "You know what I'm asking."

My breath caught again. "I..."

His hands moved up my bare sides, tickling my ribs before tracing back down to the waistband of my shorts.

"I *mean*, are your panties getting wet for me?" he asked.

"They h-have been for a while."

Jonah groaned against my neck, his lips finding my collarbone as he moved his fingertips to the button on my jean shorts.

"Have they?" he said. "Do you maybe want me to check them for you?"

"Oh," I said, finally catching on. "Yes. You should do that."

He smiled and with an impressive dexterity, unclasped my button in one smooth motion before tugging the zipper down. Anticipation rocketed through me as he guided my jeans down my hips, leaving me standing there in what I wished were a little sexier than grey and pink cotton polka dot panties.

But based on Jonah's reaction, they were fine as they were.

"Perfect," he whispered.

I shifted, delighted but self-conscious. "Can we do yours now?"

"Hell yeah."

Once his pants were gone, I couldn't take my eyes off him. His body was sculpted in a way that was enticing and breathtaking and enthralling. Of course, his chest was great, but his legs... wow. He wore black boxer-briefs, the leg holes tight around muscular thighs that looked every bit as powerful as I'd imagined, and they were slung low enough on his hips that I could see a V pointing beneath the waistband.

Oh, and his cock was hard.

Like, really hard. And really big. Which I could tell, since he was standing there in black boxer-briefs that were bulging out with a big, hard, thick cock that I couldn't take my eyes off. He wasn't even naked yet and I was obsessed, wanting to touch it and stroke it and probably do other things to it, but—

"Everything okay?" Jonah asked, breaking through my stunned staring.

"Please take those off," I said.

He chuckled, touching the waistband of his boxers. "These?"

"Yes."

"You want them off?"

"Jonah," I whispered. "Please?"

He licked his lips, but didn't pull them down. Instead, he pulled me against him one more time, letting me feel the heat radiating through the fabric of his boxers.

"Not yet," he murmured. "Soon, Ginger Girl, but not until I've made you come at least once."

I raised my eyebrows. "At *least*?"

"Yeah." He thrust forward a bit, his hard bulge grinding against my pelvis and making me gasp. "We'll see how long I can resist not being inside you."

Before I could respond, he kissed me again, then before I could catch myself from the head-reeling spiral that put me in, he physically spun me around.

I gasped, then let out a sound that was part shriek and part giggle as he tossed me on the bed in a surprising show of strength. Not that he didn't appear strong—Jonah was ripped, inked muscles bulging on his chest and arms and *everywhere*—but because I'd never felt like I was the petite and delicate type of girl who could get tossed around like a rag doll.

Yet there I was, flat on my back by no action of my own as Jonah climbed onto the bed, kneeling next to me.

Yeah, my panties were absolutely *soaked*.

"You liked that," Jonah stated.

"Yes."

"Do you like it more when I ask you what you want or when I tell you what you want?"

I looked up at him, into eyes that were playful at the same time they were calculating, deep brown and glimmering with a desire to change my world and indulge in his own. He'd asked me a couple of times if he could do something—remove my shirt, take off my jeans—and sure, I'd liked that. I liked it enough that my panties were damp.

But when he tossed me around like that? That made the place in the pit of my torso sing, begging for more and more.

"I like it when you tell me what *you* want," I said.

A wolfish smile spread across his lips. Leaning forward slightly, he placed one hand on each of my legs, just above my knees but not quite all the way up on my thighs.

"Spread for me," he said.

My legs fell open before I even had time to feel self-conscious about the fact that I was about to bare myself to him. Yes, there was still a layer of fabric covering my pussy, but it was a thin layer of fabric and I would also be showing off the wet spot seeping through my panties.

But I barely had time to think about that before Jonah brought his body between my legs, crawling forward until he was hovering over me. Carefully, he lowered himself, letting me feel each inch of his body as it met mine.

"To be clear," he said, bringing a hand up to the side of my head and brushing my hair away from my face. "I'm not telling you what I want. I'm telling you what *you* want. Because I know what you want, Ginger Girl."

He thrust his hips forward and I cried out as his thick cock pressed against me, so hot that I could feel its heat even through the layers of fabric between us.

"You want this," he continued. "You don't want to *give* me this sweet little virgin pussy. You want me to take it."

"Yes," I breathed. "Yes, please."

He smirked, leaning forward and pressing a kiss to my neck. "You want me to fuck you. Show you what you've been missing. Teach you just how much this perfect body of yours is capable of. Don't you?"

"*Yes*, Jonah," I repeated, then moaned as he sucked on the same sensitive spot he'd found earlier. "I want all of that."

"Good girl," he murmured.

TWENTY

He took my bra off like he was unwrapping me.

He slipped his hand beneath me and splayed it open, a warm comfort as he licked and kissed his way from my neck to my collarbone to the tops of my breasts. He nuzzled them, teasing his lips along the edge of the fabric. If I'd known I would end my day in the position I was currently in, I might have been embarrassed about wearing that particular bra, but only because the anticipation meant I'd have time to wish I *owned* something slightly sexier than a utilitarian black t-shirt bra.

But I didn't, because bras were expensive to begin with and my breasts were on the larger side, so the cute bras they made were usually too small for me.

Not that it seemed to matter to Jonah. He didn't seem to care about my cotton panties, not with the way he was grinding his hard cock between my legs, or about my boring bra. The way he was kissing and nipping at the exposed skin on the top of my breasts made me feel like I was wearing the laciest lingerie I could find. And all I could focus on was how he felt, how my legs were spread almost to their max just to accommodate the width of his muscular body and how even with one arm behind me and one beside me, I felt like I was securely in place.

I'd never had a guy take my bra off before, but I *had* watched enough stupid movies to know that guys equated the simple hook-and-eye closures on the back of a bra to everything from combination locks to bomb defusal. But once Jonah was ready to take my bra off, aside from making me sit up just enough that he could move his hand, he didn't so much as flinch before undoing it in one swift movement.

His hand slid out from under me and he sat back on his knees, dark eyes gazing into mine in the dim glow of the room. There was a question there, something unspoken but clear, and even though I didn't say a word, he seemed to find the answer. Slowly, he slid my bra straps down, holding my gaze as they brushed along my biceps and down to my elbows. My heart pounded in my throat, but still I stayed quiet, looking up at him with anticipation and eagerness that I didn't bother trying to hide until I felt the cups move away from my breasts.

That was when he broke eye contact, flicking his gaze down like my breasts were magnets he couldn't resist. I watched him, not sure if there was something else I was supposed to be doing or looking at, but it didn't matter; even if there was, I wouldn't have been able to look away from him.

As he finished pulling my bra off, his lips parted and his chest rose as he sucked in a steadying breath. I watched his tongue poke out of his mouth, wetting his lips before he raked his teeth over the bottom one, then slowly shook his head as he let out his breath.

"Goddamnit, Ginger Girl," he finally said.

"Is everything okay?" I asked.

"Okay?" He tore his eyes away from my breasts and looked at me incredulously. "Have you *seen* these before?"

"Once or twice, I think."

He let out a dry laugh and looked back down, dropping my bra off the edge of the bed.

"Perfection," he said. "Your tits are fucking *perfection*. Just... wow." He reached forward and traced his fingers along a spot on the top of them, dragging his finger along my chest from one side to the other. "This is downright evil of you."

"What is?" I asked.

"Letting me find out that when you blush, it starts here—" He leaned forward and began tracing his lips along the same path his finger had just taken "—and goes all the way across your chest. Then your collarbone and your neck and your cheeks start turning red, but before they do..." He nipped at a spot on my chest, then sucked the skin there lightly. "They go the exact same shade of pink as your nipples. Did you know that?"

"I, um... did not," I said, because what the hell else was I supposed to say?

He nuzzled against my chest, pressing his lips to my skin again. "You know how many times a day you blush? And now, every *fucking* time I see you do it, I'm going to picture this."

I felt like I should have apologized or something. Not like a real apology. One of those apologies where I was actually giddy knowing that every time Jonah and I met each other's eyes from our respective bars and he did something that made my face turn red, he'd think of my tits.

Of *my* tits.

And maybe his face would turn a little red, too.

But I didn't apologize, real or fake, because the moment Jonah finished speaking, he moved his mouth down to my left nipple and latched on, the hot wetness of his tongue flicking against the hard nub and making my body *tremble*.

I cried out, my back arching as he sucked and licked that nipple. It wasn't loud enough to cover the sound of his groan, thankfully, because hearing the soft rumble coming from his throat was almost as good as the sensations radiating through my breasts and down to my stomach each time he sucked on my nipple. His other hand moved up to my right breast, cupping it and squeezing, a firm and smooth pressure that contradicted the wet heat of his mouth and the coarseness of the facial hair on his chin.

Once he'd thoroughly teased and tormented and spoiled my left nipple, he let it fall from his mouth and kissed around my breast, nuzzling the underside and teasing his fingers between my cleavage before moving his mouth to the other side. I squeezed my eyes shut as he repeated the actions there, sucking on my breasts like he couldn't get enough of them. I couldn't have held still if I wanted to; each little ministration or squeeze or nip made me squirm until I was desperately trying to push my hips up.

"What do you want, Violet?" he finally asked when my unsuccessful wriggling became too much.

"I need to be touched," I gasped. "I n-need... I'm so wet, Jonah."

He groaned against my breasts.

"Like this, baby?" He shifted forward so more of his weight was resting on me.

And by more of his weight, I meant his cock. All of it. Thick, throbbing, hot, pressed against my soaked panties so firmly that I was sure my juices were going to stain his boxers. He lined it up against my slit so perfectly that all I could do was moan in relief as I ground up against him.

"You like that?" he asked again.

"It's not obvious?"

He chuckled and pushed his hips forward, making me cry out.

"Again," I begged. "Please, again?"

"So needy already," he said, but he rolled his hips to give me the friction I was so desperately craving.

"Not my fault," I said. "You're the one who's—*ah*!"

He'd moved quickly, so fast I didn't realize he was going for that sensitive spot on my neck until he was sucking on it. My startled exclamation came out high-pitched, my hips bucking forward and pushing my pussy against his cock.

"That's right, baby," he said into my neck. "Grind on me. Use my cock to make yourself feel good."

A heady moan slipped from my lips and I clutched at him, pushing my hips up again and again. "Please, Jonah."

He chuckled. "What are you begging me for, Ginger Girl?"

"I... I don't know."

He sucked on my neck, moving a hand to my breast again so he could fondle me. "You need me to tell you what you want again?"

I nodded.

"Mmm." He lifted his head and kissed my lips, thrusting forward and making me shudder. "You want me to make you come. But not like this. You want me to strip those little cotton panties off your drenched pussy and show you how to come on a man's mouth. You want my tongue on your clit and between your pussy lips and inside your needy little hole. That's what you want, isn't it, Ginger Girl?"

In fairness, he could have said anything right then and I would have agreed that it was what I wanted, but that was *definitely* one of the top answers.

He placed a last kiss on my lips before letting go of my breasts and sitting back. I made to sit up, but Jonah wasn't having any of that. He brought his hands to the back of my thighs, lifting my legs up like it was nothing until they were almost directly in front of him. Only then did he bring his hands to the waistband of my panties and pull, sliding them past my thighs and knees. Unlike with my bra, he didn't strip me slowly, just tugged my panties off and then guided my legs back down on either side of him.

I thought I would feel more vulnerable to be naked and exposed to him like that. I mean, I hadn't been naked with anyone before. *Ever*. And I'd been so convinced...

It was almost embarrassing how I'd been so convinced I wasn't Jonah's type. With the way he was touching me, kissing me, treating every inch of my body like it was an absolute treasure, I was ashamed to admit I'd thought he wouldn't like it.

Part of me wanted to pretend he was lying. It was that deep, dark voice inside that tells you you're not good enough, you're not hot enough, you're simply not enough of *anything* to deserve having someone treat you the way Jonah was treating me.

But it was very, *very* difficult to give that voice any credibility when I was watching a man like Jonah shove my panties into his face and breathe in. Transfixed, I watched his eyes close like he was inhaling the scent of blooming roses or freshly baked cupcakes or sweet melting chocolate before he dropped my panties to join the rest of my clothes in the void beside my bed. Then, he opened his eyes and met mine, his expression glazed and chest rising and falling with slow, steady breaths.

"Is something wrong?" I asked, suddenly worried.

A short, staccato laugh jerked out of his mouth. He licked his lips as he shook his head slowly, fully *silencing* the part of me questioning if I was enough.

"Oh, Ginger Girl," he said, his voice low and heady. "I'm gonna fucking devour you."

TWENTY-ONE

I COULDN'T HAVE SAID what he specifically did when he went down on me.

I couldn't have said if he kissed along my stomach or if he put a hand on each of my thighs and wrenched them apart before diving in.

All I knew is that a hand *did* end up on each of my inner thighs so he could hold my legs as wide as they could go while he did exactly what he said he'd do.

Mind-blowing didn't even begin to describe it.

Whether Jonah was eating my pussy because he knew I'd like it or he was indulging in it for his own pleasure, I couldn't have said, either. It was probably both, but it didn't matter. He left open-mouth kisses on the insides of my thighs and the crease between my legs and my mound. His tongue spoiled me, tracing every inch of my pussy and swirling around my clit before dipping into my entrance just enough to make me crave more of that feeling of *full*.

But he didn't give me that. He teased it, making me writhe and squirm and try to push up against his face again. That didn't last long, since even as I tried to use his tongue the way he told me to use his cock, he guided my legs over his shoulders, then took his hands off my thighs and put them on my hips so he could pin me down.

"Not just yet," he said, looking up at me, and I almost forgot what I was doing as I made eye contact with a man whose head was literally between my legs.

He held my gaze as he lowered his mouth back to my pussy, sticking his tongue out and running it up my slit. I shivered, arousal filling every inch of me except the inches I *wanted* filled, the ones craving to be stuffed with something again and again, to reach a place inside me that was aching to be touched. He kept looking at me as he flicked his tongue against my clit, making me jump, then wrapped his lips around my clit and sucked.

I don't know how to describe the noise I made. I didn't hear it so much as I felt it. My body jerked, straining against Jonah's hands as sensation seared through my body. Closing my eyes, I felt my head tilt back on the pillow as I tried to figure out if that sensation was pain or pleasure or simple overwhelming desire.

"Ah, ah, ah," he said. "Look at me."

A low, whining sound left my mouth, but I couldn't open my eyes. Jonah dug his fingers into my hips.

"Look at me, Violet," he repeated. "You want to watch me lick your sweet little pussy, don't you?"

I did. I mean, I really did. Forcing my eyes open, I looked down, where Jonah's wicked grin was glistening in the fake starlight of the room.

"Good girl," he said. "Now play with your tits."

"What?" I said.

He licked some of my wetness off his lips. "You want to play with your tits. Pinch your nipples. They're so sensitive, Ginger Girl. It's gonna feel amazing."

He didn't start licking my pussy again until I placed a hand on my breast, and when I did, I *got* it.

He stopped one more time after that, when I flicked my thumb across my nipple and shivered so fiercely that my eyes slid shut. Another demand to watch him, to look into his eyes before he turned back to his task because he wanted to be watched, and God help me, I wanted to watch him do it. I gripped the blankets on my bed in one hand, pinching and twisting and tweaking my nipple with the other, and it wasn't too long after that when something intense began to build up.

"Jonah," I gasped, my tone urgent.

He glanced up, his eyes sparkling.

"I'm close," I said.

He sucked on my clit and I cried out, pinching my nipple harder.

"Please don't stop," I whispered.

It wasn't a necessary request. Jonah had no intent of stopping, which he made even clearer when he took one hand off my hips and slipped it beneath his chin. And even though I was still watching, still looking at him, still entranced by the sight of *this* man eating *my* pussy like someone had told him it would be his last meal, I didn't realize what he was going to do until he was pushing his finger inside of me.

"Oh, *fuck*!" I howled, and this time when my head snapped back, Jonah didn't stop to demand I look at him.

Or maybe he would have. Maybe he didn't because as soon as one of his thick fingers was inside me, my hand developed a mind of its own and left my breast so I could bring it down to his head. I didn't remember choosing to do it, but I did remember the feel of his thick hair on my palm, of the pleas escaping my lips, of the blankets gripped between my fingers and the sensation of something inside me cracking and tipping and exploding. My legs tightened around his head, demanding he stay where he was, insisting that he continue using his mouth on me as an orgasm like I'd never felt before wracked my body.

Thank God Rico wasn't home. He probably would have burst in to make sure I wasn't being murdered.

When the crushing waves of pleasure finished coursing through me, I realized that there was a very good chance I was suffocating Jonah and released his head with a gasp.

That was a poor decision on my part, since I absolutely wasn't suffocating Jonah. It was only once he sat up that I realized he'd been soothing my overwhelmed pussy with the slow, light lapping of his tongue. My breath still hadn't returned as he slid his finger out of me and raised it to his lips, holding my gaze as he licked my juices off it before using the back of his hand to wipe his mouth and chin. I couldn't help it; the sight of him sucking his finger as he knelt between my legs made me moan again, and a smile spread on Jonah's face.

"You okay, Violet?"

I nodded.

He licked his lips, eyes flicking down my body and drinking in the view. "Ready for more?"

I burst out laughing. I didn't mean to, but the idea of *more* just then was almost painful. My clit was swollen and overstimulated and my limbs felt like the bones had all melted and mixed in with the muscles. Little shocks of pleasure were still radiating from my core, like my nerves were sparking as they tried to reconcile what the hell had just happened to me.

I might have been a virgin, but it wasn't like I'd never come before. I mean, I could argue that this wasn't the first time Jonah had made me come, if one could count the fact that I'd touched myself to the thought of him on more than one occasion.

It was just that I'd never come like *that* before.

"I need a minute to recover," I said as Jonah looked on with concern. "Coming like that again right away might break me."

"I think you could handle it," he said, then grinned. "But you're in charge, Ginger Girl. We'll have to test it another day."

Another day.

God, he was already thinking about doing this again. We hadn't even done it *once*. That had to be about the best thing I'd ever heard in my life. Biting back a smile, I sat up, pulling my legs away from him and tucking them under me.

"Besides," I said. "You said I had to come before these—" I motioned at his boxers "—came off."

"That is technically true," he said as I knelt in front of him. "But I also said it had to be at *least* once. Maybe I wanna make you come again before I take them off."

I glanced down at the thick bulge still protruding from his boxers, then back up at him with my eyes wide. "But what about you?"

He raised an eyebrow. "What about me what? Tonight is about what you want, Violet."

"I want to see your..."

He waited, then grinned. "My what?"

"*Yourcock*," I said in a rushed mumble.

"You wanna see my cock?" he repeated. "You sure you're ready?"

I nodded, not quite able to meet his eye.

"Say it, then. So I can hear you."

I hesitated, then took a deep breath and looked directly at him. "Jonah, I want to see your cock. Now."

He opened his arms, an amused smirk on his face. "Come and look then."

TWENTY-TWO

IN HINDSIGHT, THERE MAY have been a reason that Jonah didn't want me to see his cock right away.

He probably suspected—correctly, of course—that I hadn't seen it before, on account of the whole "not knowing who he was" thing.

And I mean, it wasn't like I *never* watched porn. I wasn't completely ignorant and unaware of all things sex-related. Jonah might have been the first guy I'd been with like this, but I knew what to... you know, *expect* when it came to what was beneath his boxers. I even knew to expect that he was on the larger side, both given what the woman had said in my bar earlier that night and the fact that I could see the outline of it.

Regardless, however, when I tugged Jonah's boxers down and that... *that* came out, I realized he probably thought I would get a bit nervous seeing him naked earlier on.

Like, holy hell.

I pulled his boxers down his thighs, then stared with wide eyes as Jonah shifted on the bed so he could pull them the rest of the way off. Somehow, even though I'd had an idea of how big he was with his boxers on, seeing it bare like that was a different story. The way it jutted out from the trimmed hair at its base and pointed up towards his belly button. The heaviness of his balls. The flared ridge near his tip that had a glistening drop beading on the slit there...

I mean, I could see why he would make a good porn star.

When I realized I was staring, I tore my eyes off Jonah's cock and looked up at him, hoping the sudden nerves weren't showing on my face. They, of course, were, and Jonah's eyes were patient and understanding.

"You okay?" he asked.

"I want to touch it."

He blinked once, likely an unconscious attempt to hide the surprise at my response, then chuckled as he shook his head.

"And you say I'm the bossy one," he said, then spread his arms the same way he had before I'd taken his boxers off. "Go for it, Ginger Girl."

My heart hammered in my throat as I looked back down at his cock. I hadn't quite thought my way through to the next steps after telling him I wanted to touch it. He must have known that, but he didn't seem to mind too much as I started by placing one shaking hand on his thigh.

"You don't need to worry," he said. "It's a body part, just like a hand or a foot or your clit. If you think it would hurt you, it would probably hurt me, but otherwise, it's just another part of the body. Explore it how you want to."

Then he reached down and took my hand, carefully steering it towards his shaft. I watched, entranced, as he guided my fingers around him, my lips parted as I touched a cock for the very first time.

I hadn't expected it to be so hot, nor had I expected the skin to be so soft and smooth. As Jonah released my hand, I gave a feather-light stroke, experimental and tentative and exploratory, just like he'd said. The tips of my fingers didn't quite touch when I circled them around his cock, even as I tightened my grip a bit.

That probably should have made me even more nervous. I mean, that was going to go *inside* me. But while all those typical thoughts flew through my head—was it even going to fit, was it going to hurt, would I ever be able to walk normally again—the fact remained that I knew Jonah knew what he was doing.

I knew he'd done so many things already to keep me safe and happy and comfortable, not even just in this bedroom but in the short time that I'd known him.

I knew I trusted him, and I knew it was going to be worth it.

I also knew that squeezing his cock was something he enjoyed. Jonah inhaled sharply when I tightened my grip, but when I glanced up in alarm, his eyes were closed and he was smiling.

So I did it again, and he groaned, and I figured that was a good thing.

I took my time exploring his cock. I traced my fingers up and down, running them along the veins and bumps and ridges. When I touched his head, a sticky bead of pre-cum slickened the tips of my fingers, and I let that wetness trail down his shaft as I skimmed my fingers lightly along his cock. Jonah was watching me again, I was sure; I could feel his gaze like it was something tangible, like he was caressing me as he witnessed me experience this for the very first time.

He tensed a bit when I reached the base of his shaft and let my hands trail further down so I could play with his balls. Despite his assurance that this was just another body part, I knew that this *particular* body part was extra sensitive. So I didn't squeeze anywhere near as firmly, just cupped my hand around him and felt the weight and heat beneath my palm.

As I did, Jonah's cock twitched, and I looked up at him with wide eyes. This time, he was looking at me, and he pressed his lips together when he saw my expression.

"They just do that sometimes," he said, amusement in his voice. "It's like a... a reflex, sort of. It, uh... usually means something felt good."

"Oh." I glanced back down, not quite able to stop the smile or swell of pride at the thought that I'd done something he liked. "What else feels good?"

"What do you mean?"

I looked back up. "Like, what... what do you like when it's about you?"

He stared at me, then laughed almost awkwardly. "I... uh... Hmm."

"Did I ask something wrong?"

"No, I just... it's not normally about me." He moved in and surprised me with a kiss. "And tonight is about what you want, Ginger Girl. Remember?"

His kiss left me breathless, but I still had my hand on his balls and determination on my face.

"I want to know what makes you feel good."

He looked at me for a moment, his face unreadable, then let a half-smile creep across his lips.

"Alright," he said. "But remember, I'm still planning on blowing *your* mind tonight."

He put his hand over mine again, showing me the amount of pressure he liked on his balls. Then, he guided my hand back up, wrapping it around his cock like he had the first time and pumping our hands together. He taught me the speed he liked and how hard he wanted me to grip, how he liked a little extra attention at the tip, but also liked it alternated with long strokes all the way down to his base.

When he let go of my hand a few moments later, he tilted his head back, sighing a quiet moan of relief as I kept stroking his cock. I watched, fascinated, as another bead of pre-cum seeped out of his tip, and then another, until the tip of his cock was shining with the sticky, clear fluid.

I didn't know that so much of it came out at the beginning. But I liked it; loved the way his cock leaked, the knowledge that *my* actions were doing that and that he was enjoying it. And I wanted to know... well...

"Can I lick it?" I asked.

TWENTY-THREE

Jonah's eyes flew open and he looked at me with such a stunned expression, I thought I was never going to stop laughing.

"How is *that* a shocking request?" I asked through my giggles.

"Because, Little Miss I'm-A-Virgin," he said, joining in my laughter even as I continued holding his cock. "You've gone from saying you don't know what to do to telling me you want to play with my cock to asking if you can lick it. It's quite the rollercoaster. You're not worried about the taste?"

"I am," I admitted. "That's why I want to do it. Because if... if I don't like it, I know you'll tell me it's okay to stop."

He was quiet for a moment, then moved closer and wrapped his arms around me before pressing another heated kiss on my mouth.

"It's always okay to stop," he said. "It's *always* okay to tell me if you don't like something."

"I know," I whispered against his mouth.

He kissed me again, then again, then when I repeated my request to use my mouth on his cock, he brushed my hair away from my face and nodded before letting me out of his embrace.

He moved to the head of my bed, which was pressed against the wall, and adjusted the pillow so he could lean back while I knelt between his legs. Then, before I could let myself think too much, I wrapped my fingers around his cock and leaned forward, stuck out my tongue, and licked the tip of his cock.

Jonah gasped when I did, though I think it was only because he was surprised at how quickly I did it. When I glanced up, he looked enthralled, and when I dragged my tongue along his tip again, he made a soft noise of appreciation.

My first thought as I licked his dick was that it didn't taste bad. It didn't taste like much at all; salty, if anything, but nothing significant. The texture was strange, but the thing I noticed most about being that close to Jonah's cock was the scent. That wasn't bad, either; a mix of salt and musk, but not overpowering or off-putting.

Honestly, the best part was listening to Jonah.

It couldn't have been the best blowjob he'd ever received. It probably didn't even qualify as a blowjob. I mostly licked him, though I wrapped my lips around him a few times. His cock was so big, though, that I couldn't get much more than the head of it in my mouth without feeling like I was going to choke.

Instead, I used my spit to get his cock nice and wet so my hand slid along it more easily as I explored him. We both knew I didn't know what I was doing, but he seemed to like it regardless. His breathing was steady and deep and the occasional murmur of appreciation escaped his throat. After a while, he reached down, touching my hair and brushing it away from my eyes so that when I glanced up, I could see the smile on his face.

The sound and feel of him was enough to get me excited all over again. I loved that he liked what I was doing and the way his cock twitched in my mouth and the expression on his face, the encouraging little sounds as I learned my way around his body.

When I couldn't take it anymore, I sat back on my knees.

"You alright?" he asked.

I nodded, then looked up at him hopefully. He grinned.

"I'm not telling you what you want this time," he said. "This time, you're gonna need to say it."

"It."

He snorted back a laugh. "Come on, Ginger Girl. Tell me what you want."

I took a deep breath. "I want you inside of me."

"I just was. In your mouth," he teased.

I grimaced, which made him laugh, then opened my eyes and looked at him with stubborn determination.

"I want you to put your cock inside my pussy," I said. "I want you to be the first guy in there so you can... what was it, ruin me for every other guy? Or, no. Ruin every other guy for *me*. I want you to make me come and scream and show me what I've been missing. I want you to fuck me. And then when I think I can't take any more, I want you to fuck me again."

The laughter fell off his face as I spoke, slowly morphing into astonishment while I knelt between his legs. He stared, lips parted, and I looked back resolutely.

"You promised to devour me, Jonah," I said. "So are you going to do it or not?"

"What the hell, Ginger Girl?" he said, his voice husky. He pulled his legs back, slowly shifting from a seated position to his knees. "Where the fuck did that dirty little mouth come from, huh?"

I bit my lip, suddenly second-guessing myself as heat flushed my face. "I... Sorry, I just, I thought—"

But before I could get another word out, he wrapped an arm around my torso and tugged me forward, capturing my lips in a heated kiss as his hard cock pressed against the softness of my belly, thick and warm and enticing between our bodies. His other hand moved to my neck, cradling the back of my head and winding my hair through his fingers as he kept his promise and devoured me with his lips.

"You're so fucking hot," he growled against my mouth. "All sweet lips and soft curves and stuttering, and then you taste my cock one fucking time and suddenly you're full of filthy words and demands."

"It's not my fault your cock made my mouth all dirty."

He groaned, a low rumble that was absolutely obscene, and I felt his cock twitch between us.

"And now it's gonna make the rest of you all dirty, too," he said, and it was my turn to moan at his words.

He kissed me a while longer, running his hands up and down my body and exploring my mouth with his tongue, touching my breasts and squeezing my ass and hips. Then he slipped his hand between us, pushing his fingers between my legs to see how wet I was and making a satisfied sound when he realized I was dripping all over my thighs. He parted from me just enough that he could bring his fingers to his lips and licked them.

"You taste so good," he said when he realized I was watching him.

"I wouldn't know," I whispered.

He smirked. "Because you've got nothing to compare it to or because you've never tried it?"

My eyes flicked down to his fingers. "Both."

"You want to, though. Suck on my fingers, Ginger Girl."

Looking back up at him, I held his gaze as I parted my lips so he could slip his fingers between them. A flavour I'd never tasted before filled my mouth, something more distinct from how his pre-cum had tasted, a little tangy and a little sweet and a little enticing. I swirled my tongue around his fingertips, which made him inhale sharply before he withdrew his hand.

"How are you so fucking sexy?" he murmured.

I had no answer, but Jonah didn't seem to expect one. Not when he placed a surprisingly tender kiss on my mouth before reaching up and brushing the hair off my face.

"Here's how this is going to happen," he said. "I'm going to grab a condom. You're going to lie on your side."

I frowned. "Not my back?"

"Do you trust me?"

I nodded.

"On your side. Just for the first bit. Once you're used to it, we can move, but there's no rush." He kissed me again. "I know you want me to fuck you, and we'll get there. But I refuse to hurt you."

"Okay," I said.

He smiled against my lips. "Let me get a condom."

"There are some in my pocket," I said as he parted.

"Both of us are prepared then," he said, grinning as he reached over the edge of the bed. As luck would have it, he grabbed my shorts first and dug in the pocket, then burst out laughing as he withdrew the handful I'd shoved in there.

"Ambitious?" he teased as he tilted one packet towards the light so he could read it.

I shrugged helplessly. "I just grabbed some from the bathroom."

He kept chuckling, then put them back in my jeans and reached over the side of the bed again.

"Is there something wrong with them?" I asked, alarmed.

"No, not at all," he said, picking up his shorts and digging in his own pocket before glancing up, a sheepish look on his face. "I can make those work, but the ones I have are, uh... a little bigger. More comfortable."

Heat pulsed through my body as nerves flared up in my chest. "Oh. I didn't know they came in different sizes."

He smiled as he withdrew a packet and tore it open. "Yep. And that's why you're gonna lie on your side."

I moved into the position as directed, watching with anticipation as he unrolled the condom on his cock. Once it was in place, he lay down facing me, reaching up and brushing my hair back one more time.

"You're still sure?" he asked.

"Very."

"If you're not—"

"Jonah, please fuck me. *Please*. I want this."

He groaned softly, then kissed me one more time before reaching down and patting my hip. "Put your leg over me."

I lifted it, slinging it over his hip as directed. He pulled me in and helped me adjust until our bodies were pressed together and his cock was between my legs, hot and thick against my slit. His arm rested around my waist and mine on his, our faces just inches away from each other.

"Now just slide your pussy along my cock for a bit," he whispered.

I did as directed, tentatively rolling my hips at first, then moaning and freezing as his cock brushed against my sensitive clit.

"That's it," he said. "Keep going, Ginger Girl."

I did it again, shivering as the nerves in my lower body sparked, and again, and again. Each time, his cock bumped against my clit, as satisfying as it was not quite enough, making me ache and drip and practically purr with need. Jonah kept holding me, urging me on with soft words, until I was panting as I ground myself against his cock needily.

Just when I thought I couldn't take it anymore, when I thought he intended for me to come on his cock but not *on* his cock, Jonah shifted his lower body.

"Uh-uh-*oh*," I stuttered as the head of his cock missed its mark against my clit and ended up pressed against my entrance.

He moved his hand from my waist to my hip, just barely guiding me forward.

"Now," he breathed. "Slowly, Ginger Girl. Take my cock."

TWENTY-FOUR

I REALIZED WHAT HE'D been making me do as he lined his cock up with my entrance: get my juices all over his cock so he was nice and slick, while also making me absolutely desperate to be filled. It meant that, as tight as my pussy was, I could notch the head of his cock inside of it, holding it in place as we began to work together to get him inside of me.

Maybe if he'd reached down and guided himself in, it would have been easier, but doing it this way meant we could only go so fast. It meant I was the one responsible for getting him inside of me. It meant I was in control, that when the foreign feeling of being *stretched* got to be too much, I could stop, taking a shuddering breath as I glanced down and realized that—

"That's just the *tip*?!" I gasped.

Jonah laughed, which made his cock jostle, which made me shiver and my pussy tighten around it. Then his laugh was a groan and his fingers tightened on my hips.

"Keep going, Violet," he whispered. "You feel..." He trailed off, shaking his head as his eyes pinched closed. "Keep going, baby. If you can, I mean."

I took a steadying breath, then carefully wiggled my hips as I took more of him inside me.

It was like nothing I'd ever felt. It didn't hurt—I was a virgin, sure, but it wasn't like I'd never fingered myself or anything. But it was pressure like I'd never experienced, like my body was protesting at the same time it was eager for more. Even as wet as I was, it took a while to get another inch or so of him in as I panted and clutched him. My body existed between two opposing forces, two differing needs: the need for more, to get all of it *in*, to fill the space inside me that was begging and pleading to be stuffed with him, and the need to stop, to take it out, to make the feeling of something unfamiliar and external go away completely.

I paused, then kept going, my eyes closed as I took just a bit more, then just a bit more, then winced. Sure that I had almost all of his cock inside of me, I opened my eyes and looked down, then winced as disappointment flooded through me. Barely half of his cock was in my pussy.

"I think that's all I can take," I whispered dejectedly.

"Mm-mm," he said, placing a kiss on my nose. "You can do more."

"I can't. I feel like it's... like there's no more room."

"Do you trust me?" he asked again.

"Of course."

He kissed me one more time. "Hold still, okay?"

Then he took over, carefully working his cock back out of my pussy until just the tip remained. Once he had, he adjusted, letting go of my hip and firmly wrapping his arm all the way around me so even if I wanted to, I couldn't have moved away. I held my breath as he started to push forward, the sensation of stretching lessened this time, until he bottomed out again.

"Relax," he murmured, and the hand around me rubbed my lower back comfortingly. "Open up for me, Ginger Girl."

With my legs spread as wide as they could go given our position and his cock literally inside me, I wasn't sure how much more I could open up, but I did the best I could to relax.

He pulled out again, then thrust forward, gentle and slow and careful. Out one more time, and then in, and another request to relax.

"I'm trying," I said, my voice a high-pitched whine.

He kissed me, patting my back, whispering low words as he held himself there.

"Think of how good it's gonna feel to be stretched all the way around me," he said. "Remember how good it felt to come with my finger inside you?"

"Uh-huh," I said.

Slowly, he began to pull out again. "Think of how much better it's gonna be with my cock, with your pussy stuffed all nice and tight, so full that even when you squeeze as hard as you can, you'll still be stretched as wide as you can go, with me hitting every single little spot you need to make you see stars and—"

I moaned, and he thrust forward. This time, there was a hint of resistance as he reached the spot he'd kept stopping before, and then it was like something released inside of me.

"Oh, *fuck* yes," Jonah hissed, but I barely heard him as I squealed and dug my fingernails into his back as my muscles seemed to relax and accomodate him. He paused, deeper inside than he had been before. "You okay?"

"More," I gasped. "More, give me more, give me—*ah*!"

He pushed forward again, and this time he only stopped when I felt his pelvis pressed to mine and there was nothing more to give.

"You okay?" he asked again.

I groaned in response, still clutching at him as I felt every inch of his cock buried inside me.

"I need an answer, Violet," he said. "If you're not, I—"

"I'm okay," I said in a rush. "It's so... it's just..."

There were no words to describe it. Only whimpers. Only moans and purrs and cries as he moved his hand to my ass, gripping it as he pulled back out so he could start fucking me slow and deep, his movements still careful as he eradicated any semblance of virginity I might have had. I understood even more why he wanted me like this; sure, we were restrained, prudence forced on us so there was no risk of things going at a pace that would hurt me. But it also meant he could hold me, comfort me, touch me and stare into my eyes and take every hint my body gave him of how it felt. He could feel every shudder, taste every kiss, absorb every moan with his lips as he slowly pistoned himself in and out of me.

It was more than I'd ever dreamed it could be.

He kept fucking me like that for a while, letting me get used to the feel of his body and the sensation of his cock. I draped over him like a blanket, like a melted puddle of pleasure, giving in to the sensation and feeling, certain that I would never feel as satisfied as I was right then.

Until, somehow, it wasn't enough.

TWENTY-FIVE

I WASN'T SURE WHEN that moment happened.

I wasn't sure when my hips began to move forward to meet his. When I started trying to urge his body on with mine. When I needed something that I couldn't quite articulate. But it happened, and Jonah noticed, and I felt him smile as he kissed me and paused with his cock buried deep.

"You want more," he said.

"I want more," I agreed.

"Then take more, Ginger Girl," he said, and the next thing I knew, Jonah was on his back and I was on top of him, my legs resting on either side of his hips as I discovered that holy *shit*, his entire length hadn't even been inside me.

He grabbed my hips, pulling my body forward until not only was my pussy stuffed full of cock but my clit was rubbing against his pelvis and sending shocks of pleasure through me each time I rolled my hips. I cried out, gasping for breath as my body gave in to instinct, pulsing and grinding against him.

"Good girl," he growled. "That's it. Use that fat cock, Violet. Get off on it. Make yourself come so fucking hard that my cock will never forget how it felt to ruin this little virgin pussy."

He dug his fingers into my ass, gripping hard as he pushed his hips up and made me wail.

"Do it, Ginger Girl," he demanded. "Look at you, taking all this cock so good on your very first time. You look so fucking hot right now, split wide open for me with your tits bouncing like that."

The buildup was instantaneous and intense. One moment, I couldn't get enough of him, and the next, I was overwhelmed with sensations that were almost too much to handle, feelings that my body both wanted and hated, perched on the edge of wanting less and needing—fucking *needing*—more.

"Jonah," I gasped. "Oh my *God*."

"You gonna come for me?"

"Yes," I cried, nearly shouting. "Yes, fuck, I'm... J-Jonah, I'm so c-c-close."

"Do it, Violet," he ordered, thrusting up into me. "Fucking come, fucking *take* it. Give me that orgasm. It's *mine*. No one is ever gonna get to feel you come like this for the very first time except me." His fingers dug into my ass again and he pushed his hips up again. "Come for me, Violet. *Now*."

I don't know if I came because he told me to or if he was just so in tune with my body that he knew I was about to break, but I did. I came, and just like he'd said, it was a million times better with a thick, throbbing cock for my pussy to grip as my body exploded with pleasure. I slammed a hand down on his chest, probably harder than was strictly necessary, but I couldn't control it. If I hadn't steadied myself, I would have probably flown off of him, shattering across the room in a thousand little pieces as my climax rocketed through me.

White light flashed in my eyes, stars bursting in the dark, and it took a while before they faded into the gentle glow of my bedroom. Beneath me, Jonah was half-chuckling, half-groaning, his hips moving up in restrained but desperate thrusts.

"Oh my God," I whispered shakily.

"That was amazing," he gasped. "Fuck, Vi, I... I need..."

"What?" I panted.

"I gotta fuck you," he said, his tone urgent as he looked up at me with pleading brown eyes. "I need you. I want you on your back and I want to fuck the hell out of you until you do that again."

I moved off of him, my legs shaking so badly I almost fell even though I was still on my knees, and the moment Jonah sat up, I collapsed onto the spot he'd been lying. He knew what he wanted, which was good since I could barely move. So it was up to him to part my thighs and push my legs up the way he wanted them before plunging his cock back inside of me.

And God, if I thought Jonah was something to behold before, it was nothing compared to seeing him overtop of me like that.

A sheen of sweat covered his face and neck and shoulders, strands of thick hair sticking to his forehead as he worked himself in and out of me. His muscles flexed and released, showing off his perfect body with every movement, shadows playing across the ink scrawled on his chest and arms. When I looked down, I could see every inch of his thick cock penetrating me, my pussy stretched around him as my body took him greedily.

And his face? The expression of pure lust, of desire, paired with the desperate and unhinged noises that told me just how fucking good my body was making him feel?

It was enough to make a girl come again.

Which I did. Hard. Bedsheets clasped in my hands, body jerking and shaking, back arched off the bed and tits thrust in the air *hard*. Something seemed to gush out of me when I did; I was fairly sure that there was far more wetness coating my thighs than there was before, which Jonah confirmed when he reached down and let out an oddly high-pitched grunt.

"Fuck, Ginger Girl," he said, delight threaded through his gasping voice. "You just fucking squirted!"

"I-I-I what?"

"Good thing," he grunted. "Too good. Too fucking—*ah*, fuck."

And then I was empty, his cock gone from my pussy, the suddenness of it almost startling. I didn't mind too much, though, not when I watched Jonah practically tear the condom off and throw it to the side before wrapping his hand around his cock and jerking it hard. I watched, fascinated, then before I even knew what I was doing, I sat up.

"I want to," I said.

"Oh, fuck," he gasped. "Fuck, yes, here, just—"

He let go and I put my hand around him, pumping at the same speed he was. Jonah watched, his eyes laser-focused on my hand, his stomach twitching and hollowing as I felt him throb in my palm.

"Gonna get cum all over you," he said, maybe as a warning, maybe as another one of those statements that made me shiver and moan. It didn't matter; I was ready for it.

Ready for him.

"Do it," I whispered. "I want you to come on me, Jonah. I want you to see me with your cum dripping off my tits and down my stomach and on my hand like you're marking me, so I'll never forget who fucked me like this—"

"*Fuck!*" he bellowed, and then he came.

Hard.

The first shot of white cum oozed out, spilling over my fingers and lubing up his shaft as I kept stroking. The second one, though? That one shot forward, splattering against my cleavage. Another rope hit my left breast, a third higher on my chest, and by the time he heaved a huge sigh and his cock had stopped pulsing in my hand, my body was dripping with hot cum from the base of my neck to nearly my belly button.

"Holy fuck, Ginger Girl," Jonah mumbled, staring down at me.

I let go of his cock, looking up at him, suddenly uncertain. "Was it okay?"

"Okay?" he repeated, half-laughing as he reached for the tissue box beside my bed.

"I mean, it was the best I've ever had, but it was only my first time," I said. "You've been with... you know. Actual professionals."

He burst out laughing as he plucked tissues out of the box, then settled on his heels so he could wipe off the cum on my chest.

"That's not real," he said. "That's porn. It's about how it looks, not how it feels. This was..." He shook his head, studying the mess on my body before cleaning up more of it. "This was fucking amazing."

"Really?"

He didn't speak until he'd finished cleaning me up, then looked into my eyes so I could see the honesty there.

"Really, Ginger Girl. Really fucking amazing."

TWENTY-SIX

He stayed the night—well, the morning, since it was probably about six when we finally fell asleep—which was a mistake.

Not because I had a problem sleeping in his arms or because I didn't want him to stay or because either of us thought it was a one-and-done thing. I didn't know where things were going to go with Jonah, and neither did he, but the soft murmur in my ear that he didn't want the night to end told me that, at the very least, he might be interested in making this something more.

And honestly, I thought to myself as sleep overtook me, that was okay. Jonah might be a porn star, and I knew that meant if there was any sort of *us* thing to come of this, he'd be having sex with other people. But it was like he said: that wasn't real sex. And it wasn't like he was hiding it. It wasn't like I didn't know exactly what I was getting into.

Jonah was far more to me than just a porn star. Or a personal trainer. Or whatever other side hustles he decided to start.

He was funny and caring and sweet. He was passionate and gorgeous. He made me feel like a goddess, like I was desirable and special and wanted.

So no, him staying the night wasn't a mistake.

It was a mistake because I had a roommate who decided to throw an impromptu "Congrats On Popping Your Cherry" bash when he got home and realized Jonah and I had fucked.

I wasn't sure when he got home; Jonah and I were still asleep, exhausted after our night together. But it had to be early enough that Rico and Clark were able to go back out, pick up a bunch of "party items," and return before we'd woken up. Then they burst into my bedroom and scare the shit out of us as a pile of random items showered down on my bed.

"The fuck?" Jonah said, his voice hoarse as a Twinkie hit him in the head.

A party horn went off and I winced as I shot up in alarm. "What?!"

"About fucking time!" Rico and Clark said in unison.

I stared at the two of them as they blew party favours, holding plastic cups of bubble tea with gold party hats perched on their heads and an assortment of Twinkies and mini-packs of Pringles were thrown onto my bed.

"You couldn't have waited until we got up?" I asked, holding the blanket to my chest.

"Consider it payback for using my ballgown as mood lighting," he shot back, sitting down on the edge of the bed and holding one of the bubble teas out to me.

Jonah picked up the Twinkie that had hit him, looking at it with bewilderment before glancing at me.

"Twinkies?" he said.

"Because she finally got stuffed like one, apparently," Clark said, laughter threaded in his voice.

Jonah shrugged good naturedly and opened the package. "Fair. Thanks for breakfast."

"Toaster strudels would have been more appropriate," I said, plunging the bubble tea straw through the lid.

"Huh?" Rico said.

"I said, toaster strudels would have—"

"Oh my God, *chica*!" he gasped, pressing a hand to his chest in mock astonishment as Clark couldn't hold his laughter back any more. "Jonah, you've corrupted my sweet little virgin roommate completely!"

"Yo' we'come," Jonah said through a mouth full of Twinkie.

"As long as you treated her like the queen she is," Rico said sternly. "Because if I find out you didn't..."

"He did," I said, looking up at Rico with a serious expression on my face.

"I tried to, at least," Jonah added.

Clark fought back another laugh. "So then I guess the real question is, what did you think of it, Violet?"

There was a pause while I blinked twice.

"Are you seriously asking her to critique his performance... in front of him?!" Rico asked, cackling.

"What?" Clark asked. "It's a valid question! A guy can do the whole candlelight-rose-petals-love-making thing but that doesn't mean it was any good."

I felt Jonah's shoulders shake with laughter as they squabbled, but I didn't quite hear what else they said.

I always thought I'd lose my virginity in a heart shaped bed. I thought it would be to my hypothetical husband, who always took the form of the high school sweetheart who had betrayed me. I thought there would be rose petals and strawberries and candles and all that.

I thought that's what making love was, really.

But Jonah said he wasn't going to make love to me. And he didn't. I didn't have candles or starlight; I had my drag queen roommate's LED ball gown and some gauzy pink fabric to filter the streetlights. I didn't have morning kisses and cuddles; I had a shower of gas station snacks and bubble tea rain down for my wake up call by two men who just... let themselves into my bedroom.

I was surrounded by laughter, next to a man who was taking the teasing from my roommate and his boyfriend good naturedly, with a smile on his face and his arm around my shoulder.

Not a bit of it was normal. Not a bit of it was expected.

And yet...

"—but if he's an award-winning porn star, shouldn't he be a little used to hearing—"

"I liked the sex," I blurted.

The room fell silent, Clark's words cutting off as the three men all looked at me.

"Just so you know," I said. "I... I liked it. The sex."

"I also liked the sex," Jonah said solemnly. "But not as much as I like you."

And as my face went red and Rico and Clark gagged while Jonah kissed me on the cheek, I knew it was the most perfect, most romantic, most wonderful way I could have had my first time.

ACKNOWLEDGMENTS

My books would not be possible without some very special people:

My proof-readers, editors, and beta readers are extraordinary people who I am incredibly grateful to. Special thank you to Jason Caldwell, Nora Fares, John, and Chasten.

To Paul M, Kevin Matheny, centralsquareguy, KW, AG, PM, N, ED, KJ, MidNyt, RP, Caleb Waters, and all my incredible supporters on Patreon and in my Cheryl's Terrors group - thank you. Your enthusiasm, support, and belief in me means more than I can ever say.

I am lucky enough to be surrounded by friends and family who have read, supported, and encouraged my writing. To all of you, thank you, and I stand by what I said: you're the one who has to look me in the eye if you read something you didn't want to think about me writing! But also, thank you for not making it weird. I am so grateful for the special people in my life.

And finally, to the man I love more every single day: I love you. You're my everything. Thank you for standing with me, encouraging me to follow my dreams, and being my happily ever after.

About The Author

Cheryl Terra writes romantic and adult fiction with drama, sass, and a whole lot of... spice. Emotional and humorous, her books focus on contemporary relationships, inclusive characters, and happily ever afters. Living with her husband in northern Alberta, Canada, Cheryl relies on the heat between her quirky and memorable characters to help keep the gas bill down in the winter.

When she's not writing, Cheryl can be found listening to the same song(s) on repeat for hours at a time, spoiling her pets, keeping way too many house plants alive, and knitting or crocheting.

For more information and to get free books, visit Cheryl's website at **cherylterra.com**

ALSO BY CHERYL TERRA

Find all of Cheryl's books by visiting **cherylterra.com/stories**

If You Can Series

The Boy Next Door
Kiss Me If You Can
Hold Me If You Can
Keep Me If You Can

The Unicorn Confessions

The Unicorn Confessions
Unicorn For Sale
Death of a Unicorn

Love Across Canada

Get Over It
The Devil Made Me
Runaway
Finding Home

JOIN THE CHAOS

Sign up for my newsletter to get a peek into the behind the scenes chaos, news and release info, access to excerpts and freebies, and D pics.

(if you thought I meant anything other than DOG pics, you wonderful, dirty minded angel, you'll fit right in)
Join here: **cherylterra.com/newsletter**